THIS TIME,
HE WAS READY FOR THEM . . .

Slocum unbuckled his gun belt and hung it over his saddle horn. "Climb down, boys," he said.

Harve and Red hesitated a moment.

"Get down or get blowed out of the saddle," said Happy.

They dismounted.

"Now shuck your hardware," Happy ordered and they did.

"Which one of you wants to go first?" asked Slocum.

"What happens if you get whipped?" said Harve.

"You whip me," said Slocum, "and you ride off. Happy, see to it. It's my fight. No one else gets into it."

"I don't like it, but I'll agree to it," said Happy.

Harve stepped forward. "Then I'm ready for you, you son of a bitch," he said . . .

JAKE LOGAN

SLOCUM AT DOG LEG CREEK

J

JOVE BOOKS, NEW YORK

SLOCUM AT DOG LEG CREEK

A Jove Book / published by arrangement with
the author

PRINTING HISTORY
Jove edition / September 1995

ISBN: 0-515-11701-3

A JOVE BOOK®
Jove Books are published by The Berkley Publishing Group,
200 Madison Avenue, New York, New York 10016.
JOVE and the "J" design are trademarks
belonging to Jove Publications, Inc.

PRINTED IN THE UNITED STATES OF AMERICA

10 9 8 7 6 5 4 3 2 1

1

Slocum sagged in the saddle. He imagined he looked like a man who had been run over by a stampede, left for dead about a week, and then had fooled everyone by getting up and mounting his horse to ride away. He also figured he probably smelled about like that had happened to him. On the other hand, there was no one around to either see or smell him, so his main concern was how he felt. He concluded that he felt like he had been run over and left to lie for a week.

He had been on a long and lonesome trail. Water holes had been few and far between, and meals had been scanty. He was getting low on ammunition, and he figured that if he didn't reach Dog Leg Creek soon, it would be a toss-up between whether he would die of the slow rot or starve to death.

He had never been to Dog Leg Creek before and had no idea what to expect there. But he had run into old Happy Kramer a few months ago in Wyoming, and Happy had offered him a job, a permanent-type job, and that was very appealing to Slocum at this time in his life. He was tired: tired of moving, tired of fighting, tired of being rootless.

He had been in the middle of a job, a temporary job, but one that he had promised to finish, so he had told Happy to look for him when he had wrapped things up. He would be along. Happy had agreed.

"The job'll be there for you when you get there," Happy had said.

It was not a great job, but it was a good one. Happy had a big spread outside of Dog Leg Creek, and he had offered Slocum the foreman's job. A few years earlier, the work would not have seemed particularly appealing to Slocum, but now it did. He wanted a place to settle, and he wanted the security of knowing where his next meal was coming from as well as his next paycheck.

Suddenly he was startled by the appearance of the edge of the rimrock. He hauled back on the reins of the big Appaloosa he was riding and took in a deep breath. He hadn't really been in any danger, but still, the suddenness of it had startled him.

He was on top, close to the edge. The drop-off was sharp, and it was a long way to the bottom. He edged the horse forward, enough to give himself a look down over the edge, and he could see the town, Dog

Leg Creek. He could also see the creek, which bore the same name as the town, running east just at the base of the rimrock, then making a sharp turn south. The town was built almost up against the rimrock, east of the creek.

He pulled the crumpled, hand-drawn map that Happy had given him out of his pocket and smoothed it out some to study it again and to compare it to what he could see below. The map showed the rimrock and the town below, and it showed the creek running south. All of that Slocum could see. What he couldn't see was the creek turning east again, making its dogleg. That would be a few miles south of the range of Slocum's vision. From there, the creek would run on more or less southeast.

Along the east side of the creek ran a road that led to the ranches south of town. There were three big ones. The first one Slocum would come to would be the Harper Ranch. It would lie east of the creek and the road. A few miles beyond that, he would come to the Fuller Ranch on the west side of the creek. A little farther on was the line between the Harper Ranch and the Kramer Ranch, Kramer's spread being just south of and adjoining Harper's and across the road and creek from Fuller's.

The other thing the map told Slocum that was of immediate importance was that he would find a road to his right, to the west, that would lead him down off the rimrock and back around to the west end of the town of Dog Leg Creek.

Slocum considered the attractions of a town—any town—at just that moment in his life: a shave, a haircut, a bath, a hot meal, a drink, a smoke, a woman. But all of those things cost money, and Slocum was broke. He turned his horse west and found the trail. Soon he was riding down toward the lower ground.

He took his time. He figured that his horse was most likely as tired as he was, and there was no need to push the poor beast. Besides, Slocum had grown so used to the gnawing hunger in his gut and the foul smell of his own body that he could put up with both for a few more miles.

As Slocum reached the base of the rimrock, he could see the town off to his left, across the creek. He could even hear some town noises, but he had already decided that he would bypass the town of Dog Leg Creek for the time being. He also decided that he didn't particularly want to be seen by anyone in town just yet, not in his present condition. He stayed on the west side of the creek and rode south.

He was pleased to note that the countryside down below the rimrock was green and pleasantly rolling, and although it was definitely prairie, it was dotted here and there with groves of fair-size, healthy trees. A good country, he thought. A pleasant place to settle in.

He reached the spot where the creek turned east, and even though he trusted Happy Kramer, he was glad to have Happy's map confirmed again. He also figured he was far enough from town, and he turned the Appaloosa into the water. Then he paused to let it drink.

He thought about dismounting for a drink himself, but he decided against it. Once out of the saddle, he wouldn't want to get back in for a while. And he wasn't suffering too much from thirst. Actually, it was hunger bothering him more than thirst, and he had never liked trying to fill an empty belly with water.

When the horse had gotten enough of a drink, Slocum pulled its head up and urged it on. They splashed on across the creek and out on the east side, where they got onto the road that followed the creek. Soon, according to the map, they would come to the north edge of the Harper Ranch.

Suddenly, half a dozen riders came out of a grove of trees just to Slocum's left. They raced into the road in front of him and stopped in a line, blocking his way. They all held six-guns at the ready. Slocum halted the Appaloosa.

"Whoa. Whoa," he said. He looked at the hard faces there in front of him for a moment. None of them said a word.

"Howdy, gents," said Slocum. "I ain't got nothing you want. I'm about as broke as a man can get."

"Get down off your horse," said a skinny rider with long, stringy hair and a sparse mustache.

"What's this all about?" Slocum asked. "I don't even know you."

"Get down, I said," ordered the man, poking his

gun barrel forward menacingly. Slocum dismounted, and one of the riders came forward, grabbed the reins of the Appaloosa, and turned it around in the road. Then he slapped it on the rump, sending it running back toward town.

"Hey!" cried Slocum.

"Shut up," said the man with stringy hair. Then the riders all began to move again until they formed a circle around him. Slocum was closed in with no place to go, and he was on foot. He wondered who the hell these riders were and just what the hell they wanted with him. He did not wonder what he was going to do, for he knew that there was nothing he could do but wait and see what their intentions were. He was completely at their mercy, and they did not appear to really have any of that rare quality anywhere about them. Slocum kept his eyes on the man with the stringy hair, for he seemed to be the one in command.

Thus he was surprised when the man holstered his revolver. The other riders followed suit. With the six-gun barrels no longer leveled at him, Slocum relaxed a little. Just then, the leader rode forward and kicked out with his right foot, catching Slocum a stinging blow to the side of the head.

Slocum staggered backward, and another boot got him, flat-footed, between the shoulder blades. He fell forward, landing first on his knees, then catching himself with his hands, and he felt the sting of a coiled rope lash him across the back, then again and again, and he could see the horses' hoofs as they closed in, tightening the circle around him.

"All right, back off," Slocum heard someone say, and he assumed that it was the man with stringy hair, for no one else in the crowd had given any orders. The blows stopped, and the horses backed away, and Slocum could see the booted feet of at least two riders who had dismounted. They came closer, and then one of his tormenters kicked him hard in the ribs.

He whuffed as the air left his lungs, and he fell over onto his right side. Then another kicked him in the back, and another in the back of the head. He curled his body into a protective ball and wrapped his arms around his head. He felt two more swift kicks.

"That's enough," said the leader. "Mount up."

Slocum rolled his head to one side to get a squinty look at the men. He wanted to make sure he would recognize them all, should he ever see them again, and he intended to see them, every one. When his eyes moved again to the man with the stringy hair, he found that rider looking at him.

"Get up when you can," said the man, "and turn around and head back the way you come in. We don't need your kind around these parts, and if we see you again, it will go worse on you. Come on, boys."

He watched them ride off, and then he turned and crawled to the creek. He dropped his face into the cold, soothing water. He hurt all over. He hoped that nothing was broken, but he couldn't be sure. He lifted his face out of the water and rolled over onto his back, the back of his head now in the creek.

He didn't know how long he stayed like that, but finally he tried to sit up. He couldn't manage it, so he rolled over again onto his belly, then raised himself up on his hands and knees. From there he was able to stand, but slowly, unsteadily, and painfully.

On rubbery legs, Slocum turned and looked north, in the direction he had been told to move. He saw his Appaloosa stallion about a hundred yards away, grazing contentedly, totally unconcerned about the wretched condition of his master.

Although Slocum was gratified to learn that the beast had not run completely off, in his present condition, the distance seemed overwhelming. He seriously wondered if he could make it that far. He took a tentative first step, and he almost shouted out with the pain. Then he took another. Each step was more painful than the last, but he kept moving. He didn't know how long the horse would wait for him over there.

About halfway, with a good fifty yards yet to go, Slocum stopped for a breather, and he almost gave it up right there for a lost cause. He had to fight himself to keep from sitting down, then stretching out on the ground to rest, to sleep, to drift off into oblivion. But he told himself that if he did that, he might not wake up, and even if he did wake up, the horse might not be there. He started moving again.

At last he reached the side of the Appaloosa, and he managed to get his hands on the saddle horn. The animal skittered a bit, and Slocum nearly lost his footing, but he was able to settle the beast down. He let go of the horn with one hand and gathered up the reins, then put both hands on the horn again.

He lifted his foot, but he missed the stirrup and stomped the ground. He tried again, making it on the second try, and then, with a supreme effort, he heaved himself up and into the saddle. As he settled in, he thought that he would black out from the pain. He waited, breathing slowly and deeply, until the worst of the pain had subsided, then he turned his horse and walked it slowly back into the road. He turned south.

Nobody ever did call me smart, he thought, but then he also told himself that he really had no choice. The only place he could get help, the only place he could recuperate from the beating, assuage his hunger, and get cleaned up, the only place he could get any money, was the Kramer Ranch. He just hoped that he wouldn't come across the six riders again on the way.

He didn't really think that he would. If they had wanted to kill him, they'd have done it in the first place. They had probably intended to give him a good beating, tell him to get out of the country, and then gone on home—wherever dogs like that called home—to wait and see if their warning had worked.

He wondered just who in hell they could be and why they had picked on him. "Your kind," the man with stringy hair had said. Just what kind did they think he was? Did they know him from someplace?

He didn't think so, but he had been lots of places in his time, and he had made plenty of enemies. He just hadn't expected to run into any of them near Dog Leg Creek and the Kramer Ranch. He wondered if they had mistaken him for someone else.

The biggest question in Slocum's mind, however, was the identity of his attackers. He would have to find out who they were and where their hangout might be. This was an absolute necessity for, sooner or later, he meant to look them up, one at a time, and pay them back, each and every one.

First he had a deep black hole to crawl out of. No longer a young man, dirty, smelly, hungry, broke, and beaten, he was about as low as he could remember ever having been in his life.

2

Slocum no longer had any idea where he was in relation to where he wanted to be. He still knew somewhere in his fuzzy mind that he was headed for the Kramer Ranch, and he was still fairly certain that he was headed in the right direction, but he had no idea how long it had been since he had taken the beating nor how far he had ridden since then. He rode leaning so far over in the saddle that he was almost resting on the neck of the Appaloosa, and he wasn't at all certain that he would make it to the ranch.

Then a new wave of dizziness came over him, and he wasn't sure that he would be able to stay in the saddle for even another few seconds. He was right. The world around him started getting darker, and he did not think it was that late in the day. He also could not recall a day in his life when darkness had fallen so quickly. Then it was totally black, and for just an instant he felt himself falling through the blackness. Then he felt no more.

Some time after that, his consciousness began to reassert itself, but slowly, only a little at a time. He was aware of being handled, being lifted, being moved. He felt himself being deposited on a hard surface, wood, like a wooden floor. It started to move. A wagon bed. He drifted back into a deep sleep.

When the movement stopped, he was again aware, but as from a distance and through a thick fog. He heard distant voices, and he was moved again, carried, and at last he was laid out on something soft, a bed. The whole thing was like a dream, and the softness beneath him made it all the more dreamlike.

Someone undressed him and bathed him with soft, gentle hands, rolled him over, and bathed him all over his body. The cuts and scratches were being tended to. He could tell that. Then he was covered with something soft and smooth, and he slept.

When he came fully awake, he was conscious first of pain, intense pain all over his battered body, next of a powerful gut-wrenching hunger, then of the fact of his own nakedness under the covers. Finally, he was conscious of his surroundings. He was lying in a large bed in a nicely furnished bedroom, and the sun was low in the sky. He couldn't actually see the sun, but he could tell by the dimness of the light in the room and the gray of the sky, which he could see through the curtainless window.

He tried to sort out the events of the day and bring himself up to present time. He had ridden down off the rimrock, past the town of Dog Leg Creek, across the creek itself and onto the road. He had been surprised and surrounded by six armed men, then savagely beaten. He had managed to get himself back to his horse and back in the saddle. Then he had ridden, he hoped, toward the Kramer Ranch for a while, but for just how long, he did not know.

He had passed out and fallen from his horse. Then, obviously, someone had found him, picked him up, and taken him somewhere. Whoever that someone was had put him in bed, undressed him, bathed him and tended his wounds. He had passed the rest of the day asleep or in some kind of state of semiconsciousness, for the sun was already low in the sky.

He brought a hand out from under the covers and felt the side of his head. It was tender there where one of the gang on the road had kicked him. It was also bandaged. His hand slid down from the bandage and inadvertently rubbed the side of his face. It was smooth. Someone had also given him a shave. His stomach twisted and gurgled, and wished that the someone would come back and feed him.

Then the bedroom door was pushed open from the other side, and a round, bald head with a mustached face peered into the room.

"Happy?" said Slocum.

"Slocum, you're awake," said Happy Kramer, pushing the door the rest of the way open and striding into the room. "Damn. We were worried about you, partner. How you feeling?"

"Like I been chewed up and spit out," said Slocum. "How'd I get here?"

"Couple of my boys found you out on the road and brought you in," said Kramer. "We couldn't get nothing out of you. You were out cold."

"Yeah. I haven't slept through an afternoon like that for a long time. Maybe never."

"An afternoon?" said Kramer. "Hell. You slept all day and all night. It's morning, Slocum."

"Well, I'll be damned. No wonder I'm so ferocious hungry."

"Yeah. I figured you would be. I'll go get Joy to fix you some grub. We can talk later about what happened to you. Get you fed first."

Slocum started to stop Kramer and ask him for some clothes. He also wanted to ask who Joy was, but he didn't have the energy to stop the man from rushing on out of the room. He relaxed into the pillow, heaved a sigh, and waited.

He didn't have to wait long. A young woman came into the room carrying a tray. There was nothing on the tray but a cup of coffee. Slocum could see the steam coming up from the cup, and it looked inviting, but he also looked at the girl. No more than twenty-four, he guessed, she had a round face with big blue eyes and a small but full-lipped, pouty mouth. Her light, not quite blond hair was long and curly. She wore a man's shirt, and the tail was tucked into tight-fitting jeans.

"Good morning," she said. "I'm glad to see that you're awake."

"I'm glad to be awake," said Slocum. "Glad to be alive, actually."

"Yeah," she said. "You took quite a beating. I hear you're hungry."

"I sure am."

"Well, you can start with coffee. Sit up and I'll put this tray on your lap."

Slocum lifted his head and shoulders with a groan and scootched himself backward until he was almost in a sitting position. He leaned against the headboard, and she put the tray down across his thighs.

"Black?" she said.

"What?"

"Your coffee. You take it black?"

"Oh. Yeah. Thanks."

"I know you," she said. "You're Slocum. Do you have a first name?"

"I don't use it much," said Slocum, "but it's John."

"Well, John, I'm Joy Kramer. I'll be back in a few minutes with your breakfast."

As Joy walked out of the room, Slocum watched her lovely ass bounce, one cheek at a time, inside the tightly stretched denim. Slocum thought that she was well named, and he wondered who she was in relation to old Happy. Wife? Daughter? He hoped that she was not Happy's wife, but then, it really wasn't any of his business, and, for the kinds of thoughts he was having, and the feelings that would follow as soon as he was once again well fed, he could always ride into town and find a whorehouse. He picked up the cup and sipped hot coffee.

He had just finished the coffee when Joy came back into the room. She was carrying a second tray, and it contained a plate of pancakes and another of fried eggs, fried potatoes, and a well-done steak. There were biscuits and a bowl of gravy. There was also a coffeepot on the tray. She put it down on a bedside table and began transferring the plates to the tray on Slocum's thighs.

"Chow down," she said. "There's plenty more where this came from." She picked up the coffeepot and refilled Slocum's cup. He was already chewing. "In case you were wondering," she said, "Happy's my uncle, my father's brother."

Slocum, of course, had been wondering, but in response to her statement, he only muttered and nodded. He had a mouthful of food. Just then Happy came back into the room.

"You're looking better already, Slocum," he said.

Slocum swallowed.

"I'm starting to feel better," he said. "Say, who were those guys who jumped me?"

"I don't know," said Happy. "How would I know? I didn't see them. I wasn't there. Remember?

A couple of my boys found you out on the road."

"I don't know anyone in these parts except you, Happy," said Slocum. "I rode in for the first time and didn't even stop in town. Then six guys come out of the trees and surround me with their guns out. They pounded on me for a while, then they tell me, 'Go back where you came from. We don't need your kind around here.' What'd they mean by that?"

"I don't know," said Kramer.

"What did they look like, John?" asked Joy.

"John?" said Kramer.

"Well, it's his name," said Joy. "So?"

Kramer shrugged.

"The ringleader was skinny," said Slocum. "He had a long skinny face and shoulder-length hair, real stringy. And he's trying to have a mustache, but it's more like long peach fuzz. Beady eyes. An ugly sneer on his face."

"That sounds like Harley Church," said Joy.

"Church?" said Slocum.

"Yeah," said Joy. "He's the foreman at our neighbor's ranch across the creek, the Fuller Ranch. The others were most likely some of the hands from over there."

"Why would ranch hands jump me like that?"

"They probably figured out who you were," she said, "that you were headed here."

"Joy," said Kramer, "ain't you got something to do? Out in the kitchen? Or outside? Let the man eat his breakfast in peace."

Joy started to protest, humphed instead, and turned and flounced out of the room. Slocum watched her ass with great interest. When she had disappeared, he turned his attention back to his meal.

"You, uh, you just rest easy now," said Kramer. "Take all the time you need. There's no hurry. You're on the payroll already. Have been since they brought you onto the place yesterday. But there ain't no hurry for you to get out and about. I want you mended real good. Good as new. So just relax."

And don't ask too many questions? Slocum thought. He kept eating. Well, all right. For now. He knew that if he didn't like the setup at this place, he wouldn't be able to just ride out, not yet, so he might as well play along for the time being. Sooner or later, he'd get his strength back, and he'd get the answers he wanted. Then, if he didn't like the answers, he'd collect his wages, pack up, and ride out.

"Anything you need, Slocum," said Kramer, "you just call out. Anything. Right now, I've got to go out to the east range and check on a little problem out there. I'll see you when I get back. Rest easy. Okay? Rest easy."

Happy Kramer left the room, and he left Slocum with more questions than he'd had before. He'd gotten one answer. The ringleader was Harley Church, foreman of the Fuller Ranch. But why had Church and his cronies attacked Slocum and tried to scare him out of the country? And perhaps even more to the point, why did Happy Kramer not want to talk about it?

He finished his meal and was twisting, trying to reach the coffeepot, which still sat on the tray on the bedside table, when Joy came back in.

"Here," she said. "I'll get that."

Slocum fell back into the pillow with a groan.

"Thanks," he said. "And thanks for the food. It was real good, and I feel a whole lot better. I can't remember a time when I was any hungrier than this morning."

She handed him a full coffee cup.

"I'm glad you liked it," she said, "and I'm glad you feel better. Did you get enough?"

"Oh yes," he said. "More than enough."

"Then I'll take the tray," she said, and she picked it up off his thighs and moved it to the table. She glanced back over her shoulder and caught him looking at her ass. She smiled. Then she sat down on the edge of the bed and put a hand on his head. Her hand was cool, but it had the opposite effect on Slocum. He felt the heat rush through his body.

"How do you feel?" she asked.

"Sore," he said, "but better. At least nothing was broken. Just a lot of cuts and bruises. Do you, uh, do you think you could find me some clothes? At least a pair of britches. I need to get up and go out back."

"No, you don't," she said.

"Don't what? Need britches or need to go?"

"You don't need to go out back, because we got

indoor plumbing," she said, "right through that door."

She indicated a door right there in the bedroom. Slocum had taken it to be a door to a clothes closet.

"Inside?" he said.

"That's right. We're the most up-to-date folks in these parts. And since you don't need to go outside, you don't need britches."

"Well then," he said, "are you just going to sit there and watch me uncover myself and walk across the room stark naked?"

"Why not?" she said. "I've already seen everything you've got."

"You?" he said. "You undressed me."

"That's right."

"And washed me?"

"All over."

"Well . . . all right then," he said, and he flung back the covers to reveal himself, sat up on the edge of the bed, stood up carefully to test his legs, then headed for the room to check out the indoor plumbing.

3

Everything was in there all right. He was amazed. He knew that such things existed, but he had never made use of them before. In addition to the pot with the chain-pull tank overhead, there was a basin with pipes and a spigot for running water. There were fresh towels hanging on the wall, and there was a cabinet with a mirror on its door at just about face level. Slocum had to lean forward a little to see his face in it.

He made use of the fancy facilities, washed up, and rinsed his mouth thoroughly. In spite of the bruises and stiffness and soreness his body still suffered from, all this ablution did make him feel much improved. He checked himself in the mirror one last time, testing the smoothness of his cheeks with his hand and slicking down his hair a bit. Then he straightened himself up and opened the door to step boldly back into the room.

Joy was in the bed, the covers pulled up to her chin. She smiled at him, an impish smile. He walked across the floor in heavy anticipation, and when he noticed her clothing tossed casually on the chair beside the bed, his hopes were more than bolstered.

"Do you mind?" she asked.

"No," he said. "Not a bit."

She reached one bare arm out to flip back the covers on his side of the bed.

"Come on in then," she said.

Slocum crawled in under the covers and snuggled toward her. The touch of her flesh against his drove him nearly wild. It had been a long time. He rolled over on his side to face her, his right arm reaching around her, his hand stroking her smooth, lovely back. Their lips met and opened, and her tongue shot out to tickle the roof of his mouth.

Slocum slid his hand down her back until he found the crack of her ass. Then he let his fingers trail their way down to her tight little hole and tickle it. She moaned and lifted her left leg. Slocum moved his hand around front in order to probe her wet crotch.

At about the same time, her left hand found his hard cock and gripped it tight. It pulsed, trying to buck its way out of her fist.

"I wondered what this would be like when it came back to life," she said.

"Let's put it to work," suggested Slocum.

Joy rolled onto her back, pulling him after her and spreading her thighs. He moved on top of her, his legs between hers, and she guided the throbbing cock into her smooth and waiting cunt.

"Ahhh," Slocum sighed with ecstatic relief. He fought back an urge to start humping her furiously, and instead eased himself forward, slowly, deeper and deeper. Joy gripped the cheeks of his ass hard, one in each hand, and her fingernails dug into his flesh. At the same time, she thrust her hips upward and pulled him down, into her. She groaned with intense pleasure.

Then, "Fuck me, John," she said. "Fuck me hard."

He drove into her again and again, harder, faster with each lunge. And she responded in kind, ramming her pelvis upward against his downward plunge with a loud smack, smack, smack.

His balls were anxious to explode, but he did not want to disappoint Joy by ejaculating too soon. He slowed his pace, then pushed into her slow and deep and held it for a moment. Then he forced his arms underneath her shoulders and rolled over onto his back, pulling her on top. She flung the covers back and sat up, so that she was on her knees, astride his middle. His cock was still deep inside her.

Slocum looked up at her, seeing her naked body for the first time. She was lovely, with smooth white skin and curves in all the right places. A little more weight would have made her plump, but as she was, he thought, she was just right. He reached up with both hands, getting a ripe round breast in each, and he squeezed gently. She shuddered all over and made a sound halfway between a coo and a giggle.

Then she rocked her hips forward, sliding her bare butt on his bare thighs, and then she rocked back. Faster and faster she rocked, until she finally stopped abruptly and shouted out with intense pleasure. She collapsed forward, her breasts pressed against his chest. She seemed worn out, exhausted. At last she lifted her head and kissed him, her tongue once again probing the inside of his mouth. Then, backing off with an almost wicked smile, she sat up and repeated the whole process.

The sixth time she roared with delight and collapsed on his chest, Slocum nibbled at her ear, then whispered into it.

"You're a greedy little thing," he said. "When's it going to be my turn?"

"Right now," she said. She sat up again, looking lasciviously into his eyes, and slowly she raised her hips until his engorged cock slipped loose and slapped against his belly. On her hands and knees, she moved backward until her face was just above his glistening tool, slimy with her juices. She gripped it tight in one hand and lifted it toward her open lips. Slocum's heart pounded furiously in his chest.

Joy's tongue shot out and flicked the head of Slocum's cock, and Slocum flinched with a pleasure that was very close to pain. Then her lips clamped hard around the head. She stayed there for a moment, run-

ning her tongue back and forth and around, driving
him crazy. At last she sucked deeply, lowering her
head at the same time, and Slocum was amazed to
discover that she was able to take in the entire length
of his rod.

Unable to lie still and let her do the work, he began
to flex the muscles of his buttocks to make short and
quick upward thrusts. It didn't take many. He felt
everything in his crotch come loose with a gush. He
felt it shoot again and again. And he could tell by the
slurping and gulping sounds that came from the
mouth and throat of Joy that she was hungrily sucking
and swallowing it all. At last, spent, he lay still.

A moment later, she slowly slid the softening cock
out of her mouth and lay her head on his thigh. Neither of them said a word. Breathing softly and deeply
and evenly, they both fell asleep.

Slocum woke up to the sound of a slamming door.

"Oh God!" exclaimed Joy. She vaulted out of bed,
jerked the covers up over Slocum, grabbed her clothes
off the chair, and ran for the indoor john, closing the
door behind her. Slocum could hear the sound of footsteps in the other room. They came closer, and in a
moment, Happy Kramer poked his face in through the
door.

"Slocum?" he said.

"Come in, Happy."

"You're looking better," said Happy.

"A good meal works wonders," said Slocum.

"Yeah," said Happy. "I reckon it does at that."

He walked to the chair beside the bed and sat down.

"You ready to tell me what's going on around here, Happy?" Slocum asked.

"What do you mean? Say, where's Joy? Have you seen her?"

Kramer's question was answered by the pull of the chain in the little room. He blushed a dark purple.

"Oh," he said. "Uh, what was it you asked me about?"

"If you're ready to tell me what the hell's going on around here," said Slocum. "You know what I asked, and you know what I'm talking about. Cut the bullshit and fill me in."

The door to the inside john opened, and Joy stepped out into the bedroom.

"I think that's a good idea, Happy," she said. "What did you tell John when you offered him this job, anyway?"

"Well, I, uh—"

"He told me he had a real going concern here," said Slocum, "but he needed a good foreman."

"Is that all?" asked Joy, incredulous.

"Well, yeah, I told him that," said Happy, "and it's true. It's the richest ranch in the territory."

"I'd say so," said Slocum, "judging from the furnishings of that little room in there, but I've got a feeling there's something more. Something you didn't tell me."

"In the first place," said Joy, "we don't need a foreman. Sully Nolan's as good as they come, and I haven't heard anything to indicate that Sully's ready to quit.''

"Well, it's a big ranch," said Happy, "and Sully could use some help."

"I've never heard of two foremen on one spread," said Slocum. "Be too much like two women in one kitchen. Someone's got to be the boss."

"I'm the boss," said Happy.

"Happy," said Joy, placing her hands on her hips, "if you don't tell him the truth, I will. You brought the man out here under false pretenses, and I don't like it."

"You don't have to like the way I run this outfit," said Happy.

"Well, I don't like it, either," said Slocum, "so if you'll just fetch me my clothes—"

"We burned your clothes," said Happy. "They weren't fit to put back on."

"If you'll just fetch me some clothes, I'll get up out of this bed and be on my way."

"Now hold on, Slocum," said Happy. "We have a deal."

"We had a deal," Slocum corrected. "The deal's off. You weren't playing straight with me."

"God damn it!" Happy shouted.

"Happy," said Joy, "would you get out of here? Go on. Go get a bottle of whiskey and bring two glasses back in here, but don't hurry."

Happy grumped a bit, but then he got up and walked out of the room, grumbling to himself all the way. Joy watched him leave, then she took the chair. She looked Slocum in the eyes and smiled.

"I'm sorry my uncle lied to you," she said. "He's just so desperate, but that's no excuse. He didn't get you here to be foreman."

"What then?" asked Slocum.

"A gunfighter."

Slocum sucked in a deep breath and let it back out in the form of a long, loud sigh.

"That's about how I had it figured," he said. "Those men who met me on the road? That Church and his buddies?"

"From the Fuller Ranch," said Joy. "Yes. They're the problem. We got along just fine with old Jim Fuller up until a few months ago. Then things started happening."

"Like what?"

"A few head of missing cattle. Just a few. A fence cut. A fight between some of his boys and some of ours. A range fire one time. And lately more cattle missing. Just before Happy made that trip to Wyoming where he hired you, there were guns fired on both sides. Fortunately, no one was hit, but it's gotten to the point where anytime anyone from the Fuller Ranch sees any of our boys, there's apt to be shooting."

"It sounds to me like you're on the verge of a full-scale range war," said Slocum.

"That's just what we're afraid of," said Joy. "And that's what I was hired to deal with."

"Yeah."

Happy came back into the room just then. He had a bottle in one hand and two glasses in the other. He put the glasses down on a table and poured them full. Taking one in each hand, he carried them to the bedside and handed one to Slocum. Slocum was aggravated with Happy, but he wanted the whiskey. He hadn't had a drink of good whiskey for some time. He took it.

"I wish you'd told me all this in the first place," he said to Happy.

"Would you have taken the job?"

"No."

"That's why I didn't tell you."

Slocum took a drink of the whiskey and felt it burn its way down his throat. It was good whiskey.

"Well," he said, "I ain't taking it now, either."

"What else you got?" asked Happy.

"Nothing."

"You got any money?"

"No, but I figure you owe me some for bringing me all the way out here the way you did."

"Suppose I give you a few bucks," said Happy. "What then? Where'll you go?"

"I don't know."

"Stay here, and the money'll keep going into your pockets regular as clockwork. When the trouble's over, you can stay on."

"Yeah," said Slocum. "Maybe six feet under."

"Maybe not," said Happy. "Hell, Slocum, ain't

nothing in this world for sure. Everything's a gamble. If you don't get shot or hanged, you might fall off your horse and break your neck. I'm offering you a home here. Security.''

''I just have to fight for it is all,'' said Slocum.

Joy reached over and put a hand on Slocum's shoulder, and he thrilled to her touch, remembering the details of their earlier lovemaking. He felt himself softening, and he told himself that he was about to let a woman make a fool of him.

''Stick around for just a little while, John,'' she said. ''Please. Don't make up your mind yet. I want you to stay.''

Looking at her, Slocum thought he might melt. He tore his eyes away from her and held out his empty glass. Happy took it and ran to refill it.

''Hell,'' said Slocum, ''I'll most likely live to regret it, but, all right. We'll try it—for a while.''

4

The next morning, after he'd had his breakfast, Slocum called for some clothes. Joy brought some that came close to fitting him, and he got out of bed and put them on. He also strapped on his gun belt. He was still a little sore, but he was getting restless. He felt the need to be moving around and doing something.

"I'll need a cash advance," he said to Happy, and Happy gave him the money cheerfully. Slocum was surprised, but he figured that Happy must have really been tickled to find out that Slocum wasn't leaving the country. "How's my horse?" asked Slocum.

"He's been tooken real good care of," said Happy. "You'll find him out in the corral. He was some wore down when you first showed up here, but, like you, he's looking a whole lot better. Say, are you fixing to go out somewheres?''

"Thought I'd take a little ride into town," said Slocum. "Pick up a few things. Start to get acquainted."

"You think that's a good idea?" asked Happy. "What if Harley Church and his boys sees you again? What then?"

"In the first place," said Slocum, "I'll be looking for them this time. They won't surprise me. In the second place, I'll be taking a half dozen, ranch hands along with me. You pick them. While you're at it, have somebody saddle up my horse for me."

Happy grinned and hopped up. For a minute, Slocum thought that he would do a little dance.

"I sure will," he said, "and I'll have him saddle up one for me, too. I'm going in with you."

Joy stepped out of the kitchen, wiping her hands with a dish towel.

"Me, too," she called.

"Now, I don't know about that," said Happy. "There might be trouble. Maybe you'd ought to stay here this time."

"I've got some shopping to do," she said. "What better way to go into town when there's trouble than with an armed guard of eight men?"

Happy looked at Slocum, and Slocum shrugged.

"Makes sense to me," he said.

"All right then," said Happy, heading for the door. Slocum watched him go out. Then he walked over to the kitchen door and stood leaning on the doorframe. Joy tossed down the towel and stepped over to stand close to him and look up into his eyes.

"You must be feeling a whole lot better," she said.

"You had a whole lot to do with it," he said.

She put her arms around his neck and pulled his face down to hers. Their lips met, and for a moment their tongues dueled.

"You mean by feeding you?" she said.

"That, too," he answered.

"I'd better go change," she said, and she broke away from him and ran to her room. Slocum ambled on out to the porch just in time to see Happy and six cowboys riding toward him, leading two saddled and riderless horses. One was his Appaloosa.

"Slocum," said Happy, "I want you to meet the boys here: Charlie Frazee, Monk Barnett, Audie Paget, Whitey Wilson, A. G. Spalding, and Pudge Camp. They're all good cowboys. Good hands in a fight, too, if it comes to that."

"Howdy, boys," said Slocum.

The boys all said their howdies on top of each other.

"Slocum here is on the payroll," said Happy.

"What job?" asked Pudge.

"What? Why, uh, manager," said Happy. "He's a manager."

Slocum gave Happy a quizzical look.

"Manager of what?" asked Pudge.

"Well, mount up, Slocum," said Happy, raising his

voice and ignoring the question. "Time's awasting. Where the hell's that gal?"

"Right here," said Joy, stepping out onto the porch. "Ready to go."

They rode into Dog Leg Creek without much talking and without any incidents along the way. Once in town, they pulled up in front of the general store.

"Here's where I get off," said Joy.

"Me, too," said Slocum. "I need to get me some good cigars. And a few other things."

"I think I'll just run on over to the saloon," said Audie, "and have myself a couple of beers."

"You'll sit right where you are," said Happy. "When Slocum's ready to go, we'll all go over to the saloon together and have a couple. That is, if he's a mind to."

Whitey shot a questioning glance at Charlie Frazee. Frazee shrugged. Joy had already dismounted and was on her way to the store's entrance. Slocum swung down out of his saddle to follow her. When he stepped through the door, he saw the man behind the counter look up at Joy and smile.

"Hello, Miss Joy."

"Hello, Mr. Rayburn," said Joy. She looked back over her shoulder to make sure that Slocum was there. "Mr. Rayburn, this is Mr. Slocum. Uncle Happy just hired him on out at the ranch. If he wants to put anything on the bill, let him. Any time."

"Welcome, Mr. Slocum," said Rayburn. "Well, what can I do for you all?"

"I'm just going to pick up a few things," said Joy.
"But I think I'll look around a bit first."

"You need any help, just holler," said Rayburn.

Slocum went directly to the counter. He selected a
box of cigars that he found there, closed the lid, and
pushed the whole box toward Rayburn. He got a tin
of sulphur matches and a couple of boxes of shells
for his Colt.

"Will that be all?" asked Rayburn.

"No," said Slocum. He moved away from the
counter. From a nearby shelf he picked out two new
shirts and two new pairs of trousers. He tossed them
onto the counter and waited for Rayburn to tally up
the damages.

"On the bill?" asked Rayburn.

"The shells," said Slocum, "and one suit of
clothes. "I'll pay for the rest."

He laid his money on the counter and Rayburn
gave him his change.

"Want me to wrap it up for you?"

Slocum grabbed a handful of cigars from the box,
stuck one in his mouth and the others in his shirt
pocket. He picked up the matches and one box of
shells.

"Yeah," he said. "Go ahead."

While Rayburn wrapped up the purchases that Slocum had left on the counter, Slocum walked over to
stand beside Joy, who was studying some bolts of
cloth with mild interest.

"You want me to hang around here with you?" he asked.

"I like your company, but I'll be just fine," she said. "You're the one who'd better watch his step while we're in town."

"Okay."

He took his bundle out to his horse and stuffed the items he had purchased into his saddlebags. He pocketed some of the shells from the one box he had kept out, then dropped it into one of the bags. He opened the tin and took out a match, which he struck on the nearby hitching rail, and he lit his smoke. It was satisfying. It was his first in a good long while. Then he looked up at Happy.

"I believe these boys wanted a beer," he said.

Whitey gave a whoop and turned his horse. He raced toward the saloon, which was down the street and on the other side. The other five cowboys raced after him. Slocum got back into the saddle, and he and Happy rode slowly after the cowboys. Slocum noticed a sheriff's office as they rode by.

"How's the law in this town?" he asked.

"William Street," said Happy. "He's a good man. And a dangerous one to be on the wrong side of."

"What's he done about this trouble you been having?"

"Nothing he can do," said Happy. "There ain't no proof. Oh, he's poked around a little, but he ain't been able to come up with nothing. Course, if anything happens here in town, he's right on it."

"I imagine he is," said Slocum. They reached the saloon, dismounted, and hitched their horses. The six cowboys were already inside. Slocum stepped in first, and he saw the boys lined up at the bar. Happy followed him in, and the two of them got a table near the bar. There were only a couple of other customers inside. It was still early in the day. Too early for whiskey, thought Slocum, so he ordered a beer like everyone else.

"I'm paying for all this, Burl," shouted Happy.

"Yes sir," said the bartender.

"Thanks, boss," said Whitey, and the other five joined him in surprised and profuse thanks, and they ordered another round. Slocum sipped his beer.

"Joy told me," he said to Happy, "that you and Fuller used to get on just fine. You got any clue as to why things changed?"

"No," said Happy. "Not really. Things just started happening. It was right after Jim Fuller hired Harley Church, though."

"Did it ever occur to you that it might not be Fuller?" asked Slocum. "That Church might be the source of all the trouble?"

"Course it did. Fuller and me being good neighbors, and the trouble starting right after Church got there. I ain't stupid. But I was in town, right here in this saloon, as a matter of fact, two days after the range fire on my property. Jim Fuller was in here with some of his boys.

" 'I heard you had some trouble on your place the other day?' he says.

" 'Yeah,' I says, 'and I'd like to talk to you about it.'

" 'I ain't got nothing to say to you,' he says. 'Except that you been asking for trouble, and now you got a bellyful. That's my last word to you.'

" 'Are you owning up to responsibility for that fire?' I says to him.

" 'I ain't owning up to nothing,' he says.

"Just then his gunfighter, Harley Church, turns around from where he's been leaning on the bar. He squares off facing me, and he hitches his gun belt.

" 'What if I was to own up to it?' he says.

" 'Are you?' I says, and I stands up to face him. I'm thinking that I can't back down. Not in front of the whole crowd that was in here that evening. But I'm also thinking that I ain't likely got much longer to live. I ain't a coward, but I ain't no gunfighter, Slocum. And any fool can see that Harley Church is. He's a pro. A cold-blooded killer.

" 'I said *what if*, old man,' he says, and I don't know where I'd be today, likely in Hell's fires, but Bill Street just happened to walk into the place right then. He backed Church off, and Fuller took all his boys out of there, and that was the incident that convinced me that Jim Fuller's behind everything, after all."

All that talking must have parched Happy's throat, for he picked up his beer and drank it all down at once. Then he called for another round. Slocum thoughtfully puffed his cigar.

"That would seem to throw a certain amount of suspicion on the man," he said. "What can you tell me about your other neighbor?"

"Forrest Harper? He's been having the same kind of problems as I have," said Happy. "Course, Fuller tells it around that he's having them, too. He claims that I'm the cattle thief."

"So what we've got here," said Slocum, "is three big ranches, each claiming to be losing cattle, and two of them pointing the finger at each other."

"That's about it," said Happy, "only my finger's pointing in the right direction."

"Just one more question for right now," said Slocum.

"Shoot."

"How did Church and his boys know that I was on your side?"

"Good guess?" said Happy. He sipped some beer, and over his glass he could see Slocum's hard stare. "Well," he said, "maybe I did say something to Fuller one time."

"Like what?"

"Maybe I said something like, if he could hire on a gunfighter, I could, too. I might've said something like that."

"And got the holy shit kicked out of me for the saying of it," said Slocum.

"Well, you're all right, Slocum, and that's what matters. Another beer?"

"I'm doing just fine here," said Slocum.

Just then two men came in through the swinging doors. They paused for a moment just inside the doorway, looking the room over, taking stock of who was there. One of them leaned over and said something to the other in a low voice, then hitched up his gun belt. They started walking toward the bar.

"Well, well," said Slocum, who was facing the door and had a good view of the two newcomers.

"What?" said Happy. "What is it?"

"There's two of the bastards I met out on the road."

5

Happy Kramer squinted over his shoulder at the newcomers, then looked quickly back around toward Slocum.

"You mean part of the ones that was with Harley Church?" he asked in a harsh whisper. "The ones that beat you up and left you in the road?"

"That's right," said Slocum. "I'm not about to forget any of those faces. Not anytime soon."

"I ain't surprised," said Happy. "The one with the red mop is called Red. I ain't sure why. His buddy is Harve Strickler. Ain't neither one of them no good."

"They both work for Fuller?"

"Course they do. I done told you that the whole bunch was Fuller's. Wouldn't no one else be out getting into shit with Harley Church. Hell yes, they're

41

Fuller's. Damn the whole bunch of them.''

The two Fuller hands walked on into the bar, but they stopped at the end nearest the front door, keeping their distance from the six Kramer cowboys who were lined up more or less at the center of the long bar.

"Couple of beers down here, Burl," said Red.

"Coming right up," said Burl.

Slocum stood up, and the Fuller hands stiffened a little, braced for trouble. For a moment no one moved. Then Slocum picked up his beer in his right hand and started walking toward Red and Harve, just as Burl put their beers in front of them. Red, keeping his eyes on Slocum, didn't move. Harve grabbed his beer and took a swallow. Slocum moved on over close to them, put down his beer, and leaned his elbows on the bar.

"We never were really introduced," he said, "but we met.''

Neither Harve nor Red made any response. Slocum lifted his beer mug and sipped.

"My name's Slocum," he said. "Or don't you boys care who it is you stomp on? I already know your names. I figure we have some unfinished business. What do you think?''

"If you're working for Kramer," said Red, "you got us outnumbered here.''

"You didn't mind six to one on me," said Slocum, "but that's all right. Don't worry about them. I'll take you one at a time, and no one else will jump in. We'll all leave our guns in here on the bar, and then we'll step outside. What do you say? Which one of you wants to be first?''

''Hold everything there,'' came a booming voice from behind. Slocum turned slowly to see who was back there, and he found himself looking at a man of average height and weight, dressed in a dark suit with a string tie at his neck and a wide, flat-brimmed black hat on his head. His coat was hanging open at the front, and just a bit of the silver star on his vest showed under the coat. He had dark brown hair and a full handlebar mustache. His eyes were a steely gray. A big Colt was hanging on his right hip, and he stood casually with hands in front of him, his thumbs hooked in his belt. The expression on his hard face was calm. Overall, Slocum thought, he had the appearance of a very dangerous man.

''I thought there might be some trouble stirred up in here when I seen boys from Kramer's and from Fuller's come in at the same time,'' said the lawman. ''I won't stand for no fights in this town.''

''You must be Bill Street,'' said Slocum.

''That's right,'' said Street, ''and you're the only son of a bitch in this room that I don't know. Remedy that for me.''

''Name's Slocum.''

''You working for Kramer?''

''I am.''

''Is part of your job starting a fight with the first Fuller hands you run across?''

''These two and four others jumped me out on the

road the other day when I first came into these parts,'' said Slocum. ''I was just asking them to try it again, one at a time.''

''Not in town you won't,'' said Street. ''What about it, boys? Did you do what the man says you done? Six on one?''

''I don't know what he's talking about,'' said Red.

''I ain't never seen this son of a bitch before in my life,'' said Harve. ''He just come over here and tried to start a fight with us. That's all. I don't know why, except that he's with them Kramer hands there.''

''They're lying weasels,'' said Slocum.

''Most likely,'' said Street. ''Red, you and Harve finish your beers and get on out of here.''

''We got as much right here as they do,'' Harve protested.

''We was just leaving,'' said Red, putting a hand on his partner's arm. ''Come on, Harve. Let's get the hell out of here.''

Harve downed what was left of his beer. ''It stinks in here, anyway,'' he said. ''Let's go.''

Scowling, Harve followed Red out of the saloon.

Street watched the batwing doors swing back and forth behind them. Then he walked over to the bar to stand beside Slocum. He spoke in a low voice.

''I've heard of you, Slocum,'' he said. ''You've left a trail from Texas to Montana.''

''I'm sorry to hear that,'' said Slocum, taking a cigar out of his pocket. ''I try not to leave too much of a trail behind me.''

"Well, you are a little like a ghost, but I've heard things, just the same. Not much gets past me. I reckon I know why Happy hired you on."

"He's calling me a manager," said Slocum.

"Yeah. I know what it is that he needs to have managed," said the sheriff.

"Well, you're way ahead of me. I didn't until I got here and ran into that welcoming committee out on the road," said Slocum. "I thought I was hired on to be a ranch foreman."

Street chuckled.

"Happy's a sly old dog," he said.

"That's for damn sure."

"You said there were six?"

"That's right."

"You know who the others were?"

"Just Harley Church," said Slocum. "I'll know the others when I see them, though."

"You want to file charges?"

"No."

Slocum struck a match on the bar and lit his cigar.

"I didn't think so," said Street. "Reckon I wouldn't, either, if I was in your place. Slocum, there's bad trouble between Kramer and Fuller. I don't know who started it, and I don't know who's actually stealing cattle. I got my opinion, but I got no proof. In the meantime, I got a charge here by the town council to keep things peaceful in Dog Leg Creek, and I mean to do that. Next time you think about evening up your score with those boys, do you and me both a favor. Don't try it in town."

"Well, I sure don't want any trouble with you," said Slocum. "I'll promise you this much. I won't start anything with them. Not in town."

"Well, that's good enough for me," said Street. He turned away from Slocum and looked at Happy sitting there alone at his table.

"Happy," he said.

"Sheriff," said Happy. "How's it going?"

"Smooth as silk," said Street. "You and your boys planning to be in town for long?"

Happy looked at Slocum.

"Not long," said Slocum.

"Well, watch your back," said Street to Slocum, and he turned and left the saloon. Happy lifted his mug of beer and drained it. Then he stood up and walked over to Slocum at the bar.

"What now?" he said.

"I'm ready to go," said Slocum.

"Drink up, boys," shouted Happy. "We're headed back to the ranch."

He paid Burl for all the beer, and they left the saloon. Joy was just coming out of the store where they had left her. She had a small package in her hands. She mounted up, and the men, also in the saddle by then, met her in the street. As they rode out of town, Happy nodded his head toward two horses tied at a hitching rail.

"What?" said Slocum.

They rode on a ways before Happy answered him.

"Red and Harve," said Happy. "They're still in town."

They rode on in silence until Slocum recognized the grove of trees in which his six attackers had hidden.

"Hold up, Happy," he said, and Happy called the whole group to a halt.

"What is it?"

"Those two will have to ride out this same road, won't they?"

"Yeah."

"I'm going to wait for them right in there," said Slocum, indicating the grove.

"Then I reckon we'll all wait," said Happy. "Just to make sure you get a fair fight this time."

They hid themselves and waited, and it wasn't long before Red and Harve came along on their way back to the Fuller Ranch. When they were close to the grove, Happy and the cowboys raced out into the road, guns drawn. The two Fuller cowboys hauled back on their reins and stopped.

"What is this?" said Red.

Slocum rode out of the trees and into the road.

"You ought to recognize the maneuver," he said. He stopped his Appaloosa in the middle of the road and dismounted. Then he unbuckled his gun belt and hung it over his saddle horn. "Climb down, boys," he said.

Harve and Red hesitated a moment.

"Get down or get blowed out of the saddle," said Happy.

They dismounted.

"Now shuck your hardware," Happy ordered, and they did.

"Which one of you wants to go first?" asked Slocum.

"What happens if you get whipped?" said Harve.

"You whip me," said Slocum, "and you ride off. Happy, see to it. No matter how it goes, it's my fight. No one else gets into it."

"I don't like it, but I'll agree to it," said Happy.

Harve stepped forward.

"Then I'm ready for you, you son of a bitch," he said.

He swung a right and missed, but he recovered himself quickly, dancing back away from Slocum. The cowboys called out encouragement to Slocum. Then Harve stepped in again, swinging another wild right. Slocum blocked that one with his left and drove his own right hand hard and deep into Harve's midsection. Harve doubled over, and Slocum raised a knee, smashing it into Harve's face. Harve stayed doubled over.

"Finish him," yelled Monk Barnett.

Slocum drew back a fist and crashed it into the side of Harve's head. Slocum took hold of Harve's collar with his left hand and his belt in his right. Then he tossed the cowboy forward. With a howl, Harve landed on his face and belly, then curled into a whimpering ball. Slocum looked at him for a brief moment, then turned to face Red.

"That was too easy," he said. "Are you any tougher than your pal?"

"I can take you," said Red.

"Come on then."

Red stepped forward, raising his fists, and Slocum moved in to meet him. Suddenly Red danced to the left and shot out a fast left jab. It caught Slocum by surprise on the jaw. Red grinned. He shot out another jab that Slocum barely avoided, and followed it with a right cross that caught Slocum high on the forehead and caused him to stagger back a few steps.

"Get him, Slocum," said Happy.

"Be careful," said Joy. "Watch him."

"Watch that left," said Audie.

Slocum shook his head and then looked at Red. Red grinned broadly and danced, his fists up and ready to swing again.

"Kill the son of a bitch," shouted Whitey Wilson.

Slocum moved forward and fended off another of Red's left jabs. Red swung another right, and Slocum ducked under it and stepped in close, grabbing Red around the waist with his left arm and driving one right after another into the man's gut.

Red's arms flailed uselessly at Slocum's back, then Slocum drove a hard right into Red's side, high up under the arm, and he could tell that he'd at least cracked a rib. Red howled in pain. Slocum stepped back. Red stood motionless. For good measure, Slocum sent a left to the side of Red's head that tore Red's ear a little. He paused, took better aim, and swung a crashing right to the other side of the head.

"Good job," said Happy, and the six Kramer cowboys simultaneously hooted the beaten Fuller hands and cheered for Slocum.

"I'd say you let them off pretty easy," said Monk, "considering what they done to you."

Slocum picked up his hat and strapped his gun belt back on. Then he mounted his Appaloosa.

"Yeah," he said. "I guess I did. Let's go."

"What about them?" asked Audie.

"Leave them lay," said Happy.

Joy rode up beside Slocum.

"You handle yourself pretty well," she said. "In more ways than one."

6

As the dust from the horses' hoofs settled over Harve Strickler and Red, who were both still crumpled in the road where Slocum and the others had left them, Harve, at last, uncurled a bit. He moaned.

"Ah dey don?" he tried to ask, without moving his mouth.

Red, in pain, got up onto his knees. He was hugging himself with both arms. He squinted through the dust in the direction the Kramer hands had ridden.

"They're gone," he said. "The bastards. Ow. I've got a couple of damn busted ribs. Oh. I can't hardly even take a breath."

"Do hink dat's dad," said Harve. "My djaw's bwoke. It hotes."

"Get the horses," said Red.

"Oo det em."

"I can't move my arms," said Red. "The pain kills me if I try to move my arms. Ow. Oh. Damn. You don't need your God damned jaw to catch the horses. Go get them. You want to just lay here and die? I can't do nothing with these broke ribs."

"Iv I wivt ai ead," said Harve, gritting his teeth, "ai djaw wight faw off."

"It ain't going to fall off, you dumb shit," said Red. "The skin'll hold it in place. Go get the horses. Ah."

Somehow, holding his jaw up with one hand and grabbing at the reins with the other, Harve managed to catch up both horses and turn one of them over to Red. Red couldn't reach up, though, with either one of his arms. He managed to get a foot in a stirrup, but he couldn't grab onto the saddle horn. The horse moved away from him, and he hopped on one leg after it.

"Hold him still for me, damn it," he yelled at Harve.

Somehow, miraculously, both men eventually managed to get into their saddles, and moaning and groaning, they headed slowly and painfully for the main gate of the Fuller Ranch.

"So, what did that trip into town accomplish for us?" Happy Kramer asked Slocum. They were in the living room of the big ranch house, awaiting lunch. The ranch hands were being taken care of at the cookhouse, but Slocum was being treated not as a hand but as a member of the family. He wondered how long it would be until some of the hands began to express their resentment. Perhaps, after the way in which he had taken care of Harve and Red in front of the six cowboys, they would all keep whatever feelings they might have on the subject to themselves.

"Well," he said, between puffs, for he was lighting a cigar, "I got to see the town. I met the sheriff. And I'd say we've got two less thugs from across the road to worry about—at least for a while."

"Is that your plan then?" asked Happy. "Knock them off one or two at a time? Not a bad idea."

"I got reason to knock off six of them," said Slocum. "Well, four more now. It ain't my way to start a fight. So I won't start any with anyone else after I get those four. We'll just have to start looking for evidence that Fuller's men are behind the trouble you've been having. When we get the evidence, we'll turn it over to Bill Street."

"It'll never happen," said Happy. "Long before we can gather any real evidence, those bastards will come over here on my range again. It'll be a fight to the finish. Mark my words."

"If they bring the fight to us," said Slocum, "we'll finish it."

"Come and get it," said Joy. Slocum put his cigar down in an ashtray and followed Happy to the table. Joy was bent over to place a platter of steaks in the middle of the table, and Slocum looked at her full breasts hanging over the meat tray, her sweat-dampened blouse clinging to them like a spit-soaked cigarette paper. He pulled out his chair and sat down.

"It looks real good," he said. "Smells good, too."

"It is good," said Happy. "This little girl's been a damn good cook since she was too little to reach up and put the plates on the table."

"Damn right," said Joy.

"Here, little girl," said Happy. "Don't be using that kind of language, especially in front of a house-guest.

"What's wrong with it? It's all I hear around this place. I grew up with it."

"Well, you're supposed to be a lady. That's the way men talk."

"Bullshit," said Joy. "Busy your mouth with chewing."

They had just finished their meal when A. G. Spalding came rushing into the house through the front door. He hadn't bothered to knock.

"Happy," he said, "I just rode in from the south-west range. The fence has been cut."

"What?" Happy jumped up from his chair, almost tipping it over behind him.

"Looks like some cows have been drove through there, too," said Spalding.

"Where at?" asked Happy.

"I'd say five, six mile down from the gate."

"Slocum?" said Happy.

"Let's go check it out."

They got the same cowboys who had gone into town with them earlier, all except Spalding, who had just come in from the range and therefore had not yet had his noon meal. It didn't take them long to find the place Spalding had been talking about. The fence had been cut all right, and two fence posts pulled up and dragged aside, making a wide space to drive cattle through. And hoofprints clearly indicated that a substantial number of cows had gone through the fence, across the road, and across the creek, from the Kramer range onto the Fuller range. Fuller's fence had also been cut.

"They didn't just wander through there, either," said Happy. "They was drove."

He was looking at hoofprints made by shod horses.

"You reckon this is evidence enough for Bill Street?" Slocum asked.

"I don't know," said Happy, "but I'll damn sure find out."

"All right," said Slocum. "You ride into town and bring him back out here to look at these prints while they're still fresh. Meantime, me and the boys'll ride on across and see what we can find."

Happy headed for the road, while Slocum led the five cowboys on through the creek and then through the hole in Fuller's fence onto Fuller's property.

"There's apt to be a fight," said Audie Paget, "if anyone sees us over here."

"Any of you want to turn around and ride back,"

said Slocum, "it's all right with me."

"Hell no," said Audie. "I'm itching for a good row. Bring the bastards on."

They followed the trail of the cattle and riders until they came to a small bunch of cows grazing contentedly.

"Right there," said Slocum.

They rode in closer, and the cowboys began examining the cows.

"These ain't ours," said Pudge Camp.

"You sure?" asked Slocum.

"Not a damn one," said Monk.

"Well, where the hell did they go?" said Slocum, not really directing his question to anyone. He rode around the small bunch to search for prints on the other side, but if there were any, they were hopelessly lost among those made by Fuller's animals. "They had to take them somewhere. Come on."

"Where we going?" asked Whitey.

"We'll go over every inch of Fuller range if we have to," said Slocum. "They brought those cows through the fences. They have to be around somewhere."

Just then, eight riders appeared on the horizon. Slocum held up a hand, and the Kramer riders moved ahead slowly. When they had closed enough distance between them for shouting, one of the men on the horizon called out to them.

"That's far enough," he said.

Slocum stopped, and so did the others.

"That's Harley Church, ain't it?'' asked Pudge.

"That's him, all right,'' said Slocum.

Church kicked his mount and started his line of gunmen forward. Slocum and his crew sat still. No one on either side reached for a weapon. Then, within easy rifle range but still at a distance difficult, at best, for a revolver, Church and his men stopped.

"What business you got on our range?'' Church asked.

"We found a hole in our fence,'' said Slocum, "and we followed some Kramer cows through it and on over here through a hole in your fence.''

"You see any Kramer cows?'' asked Church.

"Not yet.''

"Well, they ain't here. As a matter of fact, I seen them holes in the fences, too. Me and the boys here, we were just on our way to patch our fence and then to see if any of Mr. Fuller's cows wandered through to your side.''

"The posts were pulled over this way,'' said Slocum, "on both fences, and the prints all show that the cattle all moved this way.''

"Or was drove this way,'' said Audie.

"You calling us rustlers?'' asked Church.

Audie opened his mouth to yell a response, but Slocum stopped him.

"Shut up, Audie,'' he said. Then he called out loud to Church. "We're just following the trail is all,'' he said. "We're only interested in locating Kramer cows.''

"Well, they ain't here," said Church, "so you all can just turn around and go on back where you come from."

"We're going on," said Slocum. "Forward. We'll turn around and go back when we find out where those cows got to."

"Say," said Church, "don't I know you?"

"Yeah," said Slocum. "We met."

"I thought you'd have left the country by now," said Church, "but I guess you ain't so smart. I'll give you one last chance, since you're new in these parts. You turn around and ride back out to the road. When you hit it, turn north and keep going. Won't nobody bother you."

"Yeah?" said Slocum. "What about these men with me?"

"They ain't your concern," said Church.

"Tell you what," said Slocum. "I'll give you one last chance. Hang your gun belt on your saddle horn, and I'll do the same. Then we can get down off our horses and meet right out there in the middle of all these witnesses with nothing but our bare hands. Just you and me."

"They had their warning," said Church, speaking to his men in a low voice. "Hit them."

He reached for his six-shooter, and kicked his horse in the sides at the same time, rushing toward Slocum and the Kramer hands. The seven other Fuller riders followed him. Four shots sounded, but none of them found a mark. The distance was too great, and the shooters were riding hard.

Slocum didn't move. He drew out his Colt and took his time, aiming for Harley Church. He squeezed off a round, and he saw Church twist in the saddle, heard him scream, saw him drop his gun and grab for the side of his head, and saw the blood fly. But Church did not fall from the saddle. He regained control of his mount and turned it around, racing back toward the horizon upon which he had first appeared.

"You got him," said Audie.

"I just tore his ear," said Slocum.

A couple of the Fuller hands had seen Church turn, and they turned to follow him. The five remaining still rushed toward the Kramer cowboys. A shot from one of them ripped the left shoulder of Pudge Camp. Audie popped off a shot, and one of the attackers fell back out of his saddle with a scream.

"Got him," said Audie.

"Damn," shouted Pudge, clutching at his bloody shoulder.

"Whitey," said Slocum, "take Pudge back to the house."

"I'm all right," said Pudge. "Shit!"

"Go on," shouted Slocum, and Whitey and Pudge turned their horses to obey. At about the same time, the rest of the Fuller men turned around to ride after Church. The one that Audie had dropped was up on his hands and knees. Audie raised his revolver for another shot.

"Leave him alone," said Slocum.

"What for?"

"Leave him alone, I said."

Audie lowered his weapon.

"At least I drawed some blood," he said.

"Yeah," said Slocum, "but I didn't want to draw it on their range. They suckered me, boys. They suckered me good. Damn it to hell."

7

Slocum was trying to decide whether or not to ride after Church and his gang. He didn't really want to pursue them, but he did want to keep looking for the rustled cattle, the job he had set out to do in the first place, and he knew that if he rode farther into the Fuller range, he would run into more Fuller cowboys.

Church might be with them, and he might not be. A torn ear was not really a bad wound. It just looked bad. Slocum was still turning his dilemma over in his mind when Happy and Sheriff Street came riding up behind him.

"Slocum," shouted Happy, "what's happened here?"

"I'm glad you're back," said Slocum. "Glad you're here, sheriff. We were following the cow tracks when that Church and seven more guns showed up right over there.'' He pointed toward the horizon where the swell in the ground brought it near. ''Church yelled at us, and we stopped. I told him what we were doing, and he told us to get out. I said no, and he started shooting.''

''Anyone killed?'' asked Street.

''No,'' said Slocum. ''I tore Church's ear with a bullet, and another one of theirs was hit, but he got up and walked away. Pudge caught one in the shoulder, and I sent Whitey with him back to the house.'' He looked at the sheriff. ''They shot first,'' he said.

''You're on Fuller land,'' said Street. ''That's trespass. Maybe they thought they had a right to shoot. What would you have done if it had been the other way around?''

''We were following a trail of stolen cattle off of Happy's place, and it led us right over here,'' said Slocum. ''Through two cut fences.''

''Why would they cut their own fence?'' asked Street.

''To get the stolen beef on their property as fast as possible,'' said Slocum. ''That's obvious. They wouldn't want to drive them down the road and through their main gate, would they?''

''Let's go back and take a look at that fence,'' said the sheriff.

''You can see,'' said Happy, ''where the bastards hauled the poles back this direction. That means whoever cut the fence done it from this side, from the Fuller side.''

"Yeah,'' said Street. "It sure looks that way. But someone could have cut it from the other side and then dragged the poles back this way to make it look like Fuller men done it.''

"Say,'' said Happy, "are you accusing me—''

"I ain't accusing no one,'' said Street. "I'm just telling you that there still ain't no proof. Did you see anyone cut the fence?''

"Well, no.''

"Did you see them driving the cattle?''

"No, but—''

"Check out the tracks, sheriff,'' said Slocum, "while they're still fresh. The tracks tell a tale.''

Together they examined the other cut fence and the hoofprints coming out of Kramer's property and crossing over onto Fuller's.

"Well?'' said Happy.

"Well, I'd say that you was within your rights to follow the tracks,'' said Street. "But because of the bad blood between you and Fuller, I can't be sure of anything. I'm asking you and your boys to ride on back home.''

"Then what are you going to do while I sit home twiddling my thumbs?'' Happy demanded.

Street swung back up into his saddle and looked at Happy. He turned his mount toward the road.

"I'm riding over to Fuller's house,'' he said. "I'm going to tell him what I seen out here, and then I'm going to look over the cattle on his range. All of them.''

"What if he don't agree to that?" asked Happy.

"I ain't going to ask him," said Street. "I'm just going to do it."

"Yeah? Well, I—"

"Happy," said Slocum, "let's go back to the house."

Two days later, William Street showed up at Happy Kramer's ranch house. Happy and Slocum were waiting on the porch as the sheriff pulled up. Looking weary, Street dismounted.

"Come inside and set," said Happy. "One of the boys'll take care of your horse."

"Thanks," said Street. "I could use a rest. I've been in that damn saddle for two days."

They went into the big living room and took chairs. Joy peeked out of the kitchen.

"Coffee, anyone?" she asked.

"Yes, ma'am, please," said Street. "That does sound good."

Slocum and Happy also called for cups. Joy served them and left the room. Street sipped some hot coffee and put the cup down on a table beside his chair.

"Well," he said, "I've spent almost all my time since I last seen you folks riding Fuller's range."

"And?" said Happy.

"And I couldn't find a damn thing."

"Well, hell," said Happy, "there was cattle drove

through my fence, wasn't there?''

"That's clear," said the sheriff.

"Across the road and through the creek and on into his pasture?"

"Through a hole in his fence," agreed the sheriff. "Yeah. I know. But I never found them. Never found another sign of them. And I talked to Fuller and to Church." He stopped and gave Slocum a look. "He's pretty mad about his ear, you know, Church is. Anyhow, I talked to both of them, and they both swear they don't know who cut the fences. Except old Fuller says he thinks you done it."

Happy jumped up from his chair and stamped his feet.

"That no good son of a bitch!" he roared. "He knows damn well I didn't do it, because he did it. Or had it done. He knows that!"

"Calm down, Happy," said Slocum. "You don't expect the man to admit it, do you? Even if he did have it done."

Happy snuffled and then sat back down.

"What I'm trying to tell you," said Street, "is that there ain't no stolen cattle over there. Your fence was cut. So was his. I'm right where I've always been on this thing. I got no evidence. I got nothing I can act on."

"But my cows was stole," cried Happy.

"So you say," replied Street.

"So I say? You seen the sign," sputtered Happy. "What more do you want?"

"I'll tell you what Fuller said. He said he wouldn't put it past you to cut your own fence and drive some cows through it just to make him look guilty. Then Church said that he actually saw some of your boys driving cows down the road toward your main gate. I'm sorry, but till I catch someone in the act, or find some cows hid out somewhere, or find some with brands that's been changed, there ain't a damn thing I can do."

"He's right," said Slocum, after the sheriff had left the house. "Two men get to feuding. Then each one accuses the other of all kinds of crimes. It's just one man's word against the other, unless there's real proof."

"Well, what the hell are we going to do?"

"I'm damned if I know," said Slocum. "Tell me something. Is your whole ranch fenced?"

"Hell no," said Happy. "It's too damned big. It's fenced along the road and up on the north side where Harper's land and mine meet."

"It's open to the east and to the south?"

"Sure."

"What about your neighbors, Harper and Fuller," said Slocum. "How are they fenced?"

"The same as me. Well, Harper's fenced along the road and on his south. That's my north. That's where we meet, like I said. Part of his north border is fenced to keep his cattle from wandering into town, but part of it's open, and all of his east is open. Like mine."

"And Fuller?"

"Just along the road. He's got no immediate neighbors on any side of his spread. Just open range. What are you getting at, anyhow?"

"Nothing," said Slocum. "I'm just trying to get the lay of the land. Somebody took those cattle somewhere. First thing in the morning, I'm going to start riding the range."

"You want me to go with you?"

"No," said Slocum. "Stay here and take care of the ranch. Have your boys gather the cattle up together. Bunch them up and keep some armed men watching them all the time."

"I can take them up to the north range," said Happy, "up along the fence line between me and Harper."

"Make it northwest," said Slocum. "That way you'll have them in a corner. Fence on two sides and cowboys on the other."

"It'll take a couple of days to gather them in like that," said Happy.

"That's all right. It'll take me more than that to see everything I want to see," said Slocum.

Slocum spent two days riding Kramer's range. Most of it was fairly flat and open. To the south a river formed its border and kept the cattle in, and a steep mountain range was to the east. The interior had a couple of healthy streams with tree-lined banks running through it, and here and there were small groves of trees. Mostly it was open rangeland. He found nothing unusual.

His third day out, he crossed the road and made his way below the Fuller Ranch. At least, he had gone south of the end of Fuller's fence. But, as Happy had said, Fuller's southern boundary was not fenced, only his eastern one, which ran roughly north and south along the road and the creek. So Slocum might have been on open range, or he might have been on Fuller's property. He couldn't be sure. He kept his eyes peeled for any sign of Fuller range riders.

As he rode west, now and then he saw bunches of cattle, and when he was fairly certain that no one was around anywhere to watch him, he rode over to the cows to check their brands. All that he found were Fuller cattle. There was no sign of altered brands. Once he saw some cowboys in the distance, but they did not see him. At least, they gave no indication that they had. He rode on.

Slocum noticed that the land, still lush and green, as was Kramer's, was even less hilly and more open. There were but few trees, except along the banks of streams.

After riding for two days, Slocum turned north, and the middle of his third day out, he saw a bunch of cattle. He looked the range over carefully for any sign of Fuller men, but everything looked clear. There was a rise beyond the cattle, over which he could not see, but he decided to take a chance. He rode on over to the herd and into the midst of it, looking carefully at each of the animals. All of them, as far as he could tell, were rightfully Fuller's.

He had decided to continue north, when a rider suddenly appeared at the top of the rise. Slocum thought about running, but that idea didn't appeal to him. He stood his ground and waited for the rider's approach. Soon he recognized the man. It was one of the six who had been with Church and Harve and Red, the ones who had met him on the road and beaten him. He was glad he had chosen not to run. He smiled.

The rider must have recognized Slocum an instant after Slocum recognized him, for he drew back on his reins suddenly and brought his horse to a stop.

"Slocum," he called. "What the hell're you doing out here?"

"I know you," said Slocum, "but I ain't got a name to put with the face. You want to give me one?"

"Conley," said the rider, and he nudged his horse and started slowly toward Slocum. "You're on Fuller land."

"My mistake," said Slocum. "I thought I was on open range out here."

"Well, you ain't."

"It don't make difference, anyhow," said Slocum. "I been looking for you. You'll be number three."

"You ain't going to do to me what you done to Harve and Red," said Conley.

"You tough, are you?"

Conley stopped his horse ten feet away from where Slocum sat on his Appaloosa.

"I ain't going to fight you with my fists," said Conley. "You're bigger than me."

"And you ain't got five other men with you," said Slocum.

"I don't need them," said Conley. "This here six-gun at my side is all I need to take care of the likes of you. It's as big as yours."

"Is it fast?" asked Slocum.

"I'm fast," said Conley. "Faster even than Harley."

"Harley Church?" said Slocum. "I heard that he was a slouch."

"Well, you heard wrong. Get down off your horse."

"I don't need to get off to shoot," said Slocum. "Do you?"

Conley had already taken his right foot out of the stirrup. He hesitated, then put it back in.

"No," he said. "I can shoot from the saddle just as good. I was only trying to do you a favor. You'll just have farther to fall before you hit the ground. That's all."

"If you're really good with that gun," said Slocum, "I'd be dead before I hit the ground, and it wouldn't matter none. Course, if I'm just winged, I might still have time to kill you. I might kill you while I'm falling."

"Bullshit," said Conley. "Go for your gun, you bastard."

"After you, you little chickenshit," said Slocum.

Conley slapped leather, but his gun was still in its holster when Slocum's bullet tore into his chest. He gave a jerk, then sat still. His face wore an expression of total surprise. Wide-eyed, he looked down at the hole in his chest, and a long sliver of drool ran from a corner of his mouth. He fell from the saddle, dead.

8

It took Slocum two more days to circle the rest of Fuller's ranch, and all that he got out of the whole trip was one more sixth of his revenge and the knowledge that if Fuller's bunch was stealing Kramer's cows, they were doing a damn good job of covering up the fact. Of course, he had not ridden in close to the ranch house, but he figured that Bill Street had done that.

He wondered if Street could be trusted. A badge meant only one thing to Slocum: trouble. The man with the badge was not necessarily any better or any more honest than the next man, and as often as not, in Slocum's experience, he turned out to be worse.

He had heard about Street, but nothing regarding his honesty or lack thereof, only tales regarding his prowess with a gun. Well, Slocum would try to work with the law when he could, but he would remain wary of it. He certainly would not rely on it.

He came back out onto the road that ran alongside Dog Leg Creek, the creek, not the town, from just north of Fuller's Ranch. Directly across the road was the southernmost part of Harper's spread. In all the time since his arrival, Slocum had not encountered any cowhands from Harper's, had not seen Harper himself, and had, in fact, heard Harper mentioned but a little.

It occurred to him that was an interesting oversight, so he turned his Appaloosa toward Harper's main gate. He had no idea what to expect, so he determined to be ready for anything. He had ridden about half the distance from the gate to the ranch house when he saw a cowboy riding to meet him.

"Howdy, stranger," said the cowboy, when he had reached hailing distance. Slocum touched the brim of his hat and stopped his horse to wait for the other man to approach. The cowboy rode on up easy and stopped. "What can I do for you?" he asked.

"I'm Slocum. I hired on next door to you."

"Kramer's?"

"Yeah. Just thought I'd stop by and get acquainted."

"That's right neighborly," said the cowboy. "I'm Billy Riles, Harper's foreman."

Riles reached out a hand, and Slocum gripped it.

"A pleasure, Riles," Slocum said. "This is a far

cry from the kind of greeting I got from our neighbor across the road."

"You mean Fuller?"

"Yeah," said Slocum. "Well, his crew. Church and five others."

"What happened?" asked Riles.

"Oh, they just kicked me around some and then suggested that I leave the country."

"I'm not surprised. Say, you want to ride up to the house and meet the boss?"

"Thanks," said Slocum. He liked Billy Riles: a young, nice-looking man with a pleasant disposition. Of course, Slocum reminded himself, compared to Harley Church, anyone would seem pleasant. They rode up to the house, dismounted, and tied their horses to a hitching rail there by the porch.

"Come on," said Riles, leading the way up the steps to the front door. He banged on the door a couple of times and waited. Shortly, the door was pulled open from the inside, and a stocky, middle-aged man with gray hair and mustache looked out.

"Billy," he said, "what is it?"

"Mr. Harper," said Riles, "this here is Slocum. He's new over at Kramer's, and he just rode over to say howdy."

"Forrest Harper," said the rancher, reaching out to shake Slocum's hand. "Come on in."

In the big living room, Harper offered chairs to the two men. He stayed on his feet.

"Mr. Slocum," he said, "you have the look of a

man who's been on the trail. Would you care for a glass of good whiskey?''

"Mr. Harper, you just read my mind," said Slocum.

Harper walked to a sideboard and picked up a bottle. Looking over his shoulder, he said, "Billy?"

"No, thank you, sir," said Riles, "I really ought to get back to work. I don't know if those boys know what they're doing over at the corral."

"Well, then," said Harper, "I guess you'd better keep an eye on them."

Riles stood up and walked to the door. He turned back around, facing into the room.

"See you around, Slocum," he said.

"Yeah, Riles," said Slocum, "and thanks."

Riles went on out, and Harper poured two glasses of whiskey. He walked over to where Slocum sat and handed one to him. Then he found himself a chair and sat down.

"So you're working for Kramer," he said.

"That's right," said Slocum. "Good whiskey."

"You're not a common cowpuncher," said Harper. "Are you?"

"I have been," said Slocum, "but, well, you got me right there. That ain't what Happy hired me on for."

"Not foreman? Is Sully still foreman?"

"Sully's still the foreman," said Slocum. "To tell you the truth, Happy hired me over in Wyoming. I hadn't ever been in these parts before. He said he was hiring me on as foreman, but when I got here, I found out about Sully.''

"So what did he hire you for?"

"He won't put it in so many words," said Slocum, "but I think he hired me to be a gunfighter."

"Oh," said Harper, "I see. He hired you because Jim Fuller had brought in Harley Church. He's trying to balance the scales."

"Something like that," said Slocum. "Say, uh, do you mind if I ask you some questions?"

"Go right ahead."

"Well, sir, Happy's convinced that Fuller and Church and them's been stealing his cattle. He said that you've lost a few head, too. Is that right?"

"Yes," said Harper. "I have. I haven't been hit as hard as Happy, but if he's right about Fuller, that could be because his place is so much more handy to Fuller's. You know, of course, that Fuller claims to have lost cattle, too, and he points the finger at Happy.''

"Yeah," said Slocum. "I heard about that. And when I first come in here, I'd have talked just like the sheriff. I'd have said that I got no way of knowing which man's telling the truth and which one the lies."

"And now?" said Harper.

"The first thing that prejudiced me against Fuller," said Slocum, "was when his boys jumped me on the road. Six of them. They pounded me into the ground and told me to clear out. I didn't know who they were, and I didn't know what was going on around here.''

"That would have been Harley Church," said Harper.

"It was," said Slocum. "I found out later."

"Well, I can understand your reaction, but the way Fuller tells it is that he hired Church out of desperation to combat the stealing from Kramer."

"Maybe so," said Slocum. He turned up his glass and drank the last of his whiskey. "But let me tell you what we found a few days back."

Harper got up and walked to the sideboard. He picked up the bottle and held it out toward Slocum.

"Yes. Thanks," said Slocum, and Harper walked over to pour his glass full again.

"We found where Happy's fence had been cut," said Slocum, "right out there alongside the road. The fence posts had been roped and dragged right out into the road. Cattle had been driven through the hole, across the road, through the creek and then on into Fuller's Ranch through a hole in his fence. His poles had been dragged in onto his own property."

"I see," said Harper. "And did you follow the trail of the stolen cattle onto Fuller's range?"

"We did, and we ran into Church and his gang and had a little skirmish with them."

"Anyone hurt?"

"One on each side," said Slocum. "Not counting the fact that I shot a hole in Church's ear."

"That's precise shooting," said Harper.

"I wasn't aiming for his ear," said Slocum.

"So then I take it," said Harper, "that your pursuit of the cattle was cut short."

"Yeah, but the sheriff went out onto Fuller's ranch and looked around, and then I slipped all around the edges of the place to see what I could see. Happy's cows just seem to have disappeared."

Slocum tipped up his glass and took a gulp of the whiskey. It sure tasted good after several days out on the range.

"Mr. Slocum," said Harper, "why are you telling me all this?"

"Well, I ain't sure," said Slocum. "I rode into this situation blind. I know what Happy says, and I know, secondhand, what Fuller says. Bill Street says he don't know any more than I do. I guess I'm just hoping that you might have some ideas on the subject that you wouldn't mind telling me about."

Harper stood up and walked over to the sideboard for the bottle. He poured a little more whiskey into both glasses, then sat back down and took a sip of his. He looked at Slocum.

"Mr. Slocum," he said, "I'm usually a pretty good judge of character. Happy Kramer brought you in here for the same reason that Jim Fuller brought Church. But I don't believe that you are the same kind of man as Harley Church, and I do believe that you're genuinely trying to sort this matter out.

"I wish I did have some kind of insight into the situation, but I don't have. A while back, this was a pretty peaceful valley. My ranch, Fuller's, and Kramer's were all in competition with each other, of course, but it was a friendly competition. We even ran cooperative roundups and cattle drives. We figured that what was good for one was good for all.

"Then something happened between Happy and Jim. All of a sudden both men were accusing each other of rustling. And I lost a few head, too. Then Jim brought Church in, and then Happy brought you. I'm at a loss. I wish I could help."

Slocum drained his glass and stood up.

"Well, Mr. Harper," he said, "I guess there's nothing I can do but keep poking around and keep my eyes and ears open. Thanks for your time and your hospitality. I'll be running along."

"Mr. Slocum."

"Yeah?"

"I do have one suggestion."

"All right," said Slocum. "I'm listening."

"You seem to have been familiarizing yourself with our valley and looking for evidence of stolen cattle at the same time."

"Yeah?"

"Why don't you ride over my range? Just to become familiar with it, and to satisfy yourself that there are no Kramer cattle here. I'm sure you'd like to, but you've been gentleman enough not to suggest it. Be my guest. I'll inform Billy that you have my permission."

"Well, uh, thanks," said Slocum. "I'll do that."

9

Slocum didn't spend nearly as much time examining the Harper Ranch as he had Fuller's. For one thing, Harper's was a smaller spread. For another, he had free rein to ride wherever he wanted on Harper's place. If Harper had anything to hide, Slocum figured, he wouldn't have been so generous. And then, Slocum liked Harper and his foreman, Riles.

The ranch itself was much like Kramer's, mostly flat, a little rolling, crossed by live streams and dotted with groves of trees. The mountains on the east were even more rugged just off of Harper's spread than they were down alongside Kramer's.

All three ranches seemed prosperous to Slocum, and he couldn't figure out any reason any one of the three owners would have started stealing from the others. It didn't make sense. Puzzled, he rode back to Happy Kramer's ranch house. He turned his horse into the corral, and a cowboy took charge of it. Slocum walked to the house and went inside.

"Well," said Happy, "you been gone long enough. What did you find out?"

"Not a damn thing," said Slocum. "And I've been all over this country. What's been happening around here?"

"Quiet as a churchyard," said Happy. "We've got the whole herd up in the northwest corner of the spread, like you said, and we've been keeping a good bunch of cowboys with them. Ain't nobody tried nothing. But we can't keep them like that for long. In another week, they'll have all the grass ate."

"Then move them east," said Slocum. "And keep the boys on them. Somebody's going to try something sooner or later, and I want to catch them in the act. Seems like nothing else will satisfy Bill Street."

Just then Joy poked her head around the kitchen door.

"John," she said. "You're back. I was afraid that you'd run out on us."

"It entered my mind," said Slocum. "Church and them must have kicked some of my brains loose."

Joy smiled.

"I'm glad you're back," she said. "Supper'll be on the table in a few minutes."

Slocum ate a hearty meal, drank a couple of glasses of whiskey, and smoked a good cigar. He was relaxed and thought he was settled down for the evening, but then he saw Happy put on his hat and pick up a Winchester.

"Happy," he said, "where you going?"

"I'm headed out for the herd," said Happy. "Under ordinary circumstances we've got a good-size crew here, but keeping watch the way you said to, we're a little shorthanded. Thought I'd go out and see if I could relieve some of the boys."

Slocum shoved himself up out of the easy chair with a groan. After all, the 'round-the-clock guard had been his idea.

"I'll go with you," he said. "Is the house covered? I wouldn't want Joy to get caught here alone."

"Whitey and Pudge are in the bunkhouse," said Happy. "They just got relieved a couple of hours ago. And Whitey's a light sleeper. Joy ain't no slouch with a six-gun or a Winchester herself. Besides, any stranger comes up here, old Tick will set up a howl."

"Go on, John," said Joy. "I'll be all right here."

Slocum had seen the dog lying outside the house, but he had never decided whether it was dead or just asleep. He hadn't considered that it was worth a damn, but then, he had never seen a stranger come riding up to the house, either. He shrugged and followed Happy out of the house.

They were getting close to the herd when the shots sounded up ahead. They gave each other a look, then urged their mounts forward at a full gallop. The sun was low in the sky, and soon it would be completely dark, a dangerous time to have the cattle spooked. As they drew closer, they could hear the cattle bawling nervously, and they heard more gunshots. Slocum saw Audie Paget on the near side of the herd, firing over the heads of the cattle. He and Happy rode up beside Audie.

"Where are they?" shouted Happy.

"Over by Harper's fence," said Audie.

"How many?" said Slocum, looking for a target.

"I don't know. They just started shooting. I seen Charlie fall off his horse over close to the fence."

Just then Slocum spotted the man Audie was shooting at, and a split second later, Audie's shot hit the mark. The rider threw up his arms and fell back out of his saddle. Slocum could still hear shots, but in the dim evening light and through the dust stirred up by the cattle and horses, he couldn't see what was going on over there.

"I'm riding around," he said.

"Me, too," said Happy.

"I might as well go, too," said Audie. "The whole fight seems to be over there."

"All right then," said Slocum. "You two go that way."

Slocum rode west, toward the road, while Happy and Audie headed east. Almost before Slocum realized it, he was at the fence line, and he turned north. He saw a rider up ahead through the haze, but he couldn't make out any features, just a murky silhouette. He held his Colt ready, in case it was a stranger. Closer, he still wasn't sure, until the mysterious figure raised a rifle and pointed it in his direction. Slocum fired.

The figure threw his rifle into the air and fell off the side of his horse. Slocum rode on until he came to where the man had fallen. He pulled up beside the body and leaned over to get a closer look. He did not recognize the man. At least it was not a Kramer cowhand. Slocum knew them all by sight, if not by name.

He straightened up and looked around, discovering that he was in the corner of the fence. He turned to his right to ride the fence line between the Kramer and Harper properties. Another shot was fired somewhere in the haze. Up ahead, Slocum saw another figure. He hauled back on his reins.

"You there," he called. "Who are you?"

"It's Monk."

"Monk, it's Slocum here. Don't shoot me."

He rode on up to where Monk was sitting on his horse.

"Where the hell are they?" he said.

"There was one right over there," said Monk, gesturing east. "He ran when I shot. I think I might have nicked him. Then there was one behind me."

"I got him," said Slocum.

"The rest of it's east of us then," said Monk.

"Let's go."

They started riding hard to the east when a sudden flurry of shots ahead of them set off the cows.

"Stampede!" shouted Monk.

Ahead of them in the distance, someone else also shouted, "Stampede!"

The light was getting worse and so was the dust. Slocum could hardly see, but he knew where the cattle were running. He could hear them bawling and snorting, and he could hear their pounding hoofs. He knew that he and Monk were in great danger, caught between the crazed cattle and the barbed wire fence, but there was nothing they could do but keep riding and try to keep the cattle from veering north.

They shouted and they fired shots to frighten the animals away from the fence, and they knew that other cowboys were ahead of them, working as hard as they were. They did not know how many, for they had no way of knowing if the attackers had hit anyone other than Charlie Frazee. Slocum recalled that Audie had seen Charlie go down. The other thing they did not know was whether or not any of the attackers were still around.

But there wasn't time to worry about any of that. If anyone had taken a shot at Slocum, he wouldn't have had time to even think about shooting back. He was too busy with the wild cattle, too involved with keeping them away from himself and away from the fence, too busy keeping control of his now very tired horse to keep them both out from under the sharp, pounding hoofs.

They rode and they rode. Weary enough to fall from the saddle, Slocum kept astride his mount by sheer determination. His voice was strained and his throat was raw from shouting and from breathing dust. His eyes stung from the dust and exhaustion and they rasped when he blinked. Still, he rode.

He had long ago lost sight of Monk. He had no idea if Monk had gotten ahead of him, or if he had fallen under the deadly hoofs of the frantic beasts.

At some point, Slocum realized that he was no longer riding the fence line. Either he had come to the end of the fence, or the cattle had turned and were well away from it. If they had come to the end of the fence, the cattle would be coming to the mountains soon, and that would slow them down. If they had turned, they might race on for the rest of the night, unless they happened to run blindly into the bunkhouse or the ranch house.

Then the noise ahead changed, the pace slowed. The cattle in front had run into the steep mountains. The stampede was at last under control. The cowboys would have to ride herd all night to keep the cattle calm, though. After a fright like that, anything could set them off again. Slocum walked his horse forward, and he saw Monk Barnett.

"Monk," he said, "I'm glad to see you. I lost sight of you. Didn't know what happened. You all right?"

"Yeah," said Monk. "I'm all right."

"Well, why don't you ride on around behind these critters? Try to keep them calm back there. I'm going to see if I can find Happy."

"Sure thing," said Monk. He turned his horse

around and rode back the way they had come. Slocum moved ahead.

"Who's there?" said a cowboy up ahead.

"Slocum."

"Slocum," said the cowboy, "I'm glad you're here."

Slocum then recognized Sully Nolan, the foreman of Happy Kramer's ranch.

"Have you seen Happy?" he asked.

"No," said Sully. "I thought he was back at the house."

"He rode out with me," said Slocum.

"We'd better find him."

"You worry about the cattle and the cowboys," said Slocum. "I'll find Happy."

He rode on ahead, and then he was there at the base of the mountains. To his right were the cattle, milling about, still nervous, but packed together, rammed up against the steep mountainside, with their own kind pushing against them from the rear. Cowboys on either side kept them bunched. Slocum decided that it would be crazy to try to go up the mountainside or through the cattle. He would have to turn back and go all the way around the herd.

"Damn," he said, and he turned his tired horse.

By the time Slocum found Happy on the other side of the herd, the cattle were already much calmer. Cowboys were all around the herd, some singing.

"Happy," said Slocum, "is everything under control here?"

"Yeah," said Happy. "I think so. God damn that son of a bitch Fuller."

"Have you got a count of the men?"

"There's two missing," said Happy. "Charlie and A. G."

"Let's ride back along the fence," said Slocum. "See if we can find them."

It was too dark to see much. They found the body of Charlie Frazee because Audie had seen him fall, and Slocum knew about where Audie had said that it had happened. But they found no sign of Spalding or of any of the attackers, whoever they might have been. Slocum was pretty sure that someone had picked up the body of the one he had shot. He knew pretty well where it should have been. It made sense. If no bodies were found, there was still no proof of who was guilty.

"We might as well give it up," said Slocum. "It's too dark to see anything."

"You're right, damn it," said Happy.

"We'll try again at first light."

They picked up a couple of stray horses on the way back to the ranch house. One, Happy recognized right away, even in the dark, as one of his own.

"Likely, poor Charlie was riding him," he said.

•   •   •

They left the house without breakfast before the sun came up the next morning. Slocum and Happy and Joy. The two cowboys back at the bunkhouse were left behind, just to make sure that nothing happened to the house, bunkhouse, or corral while they were gone. By the time they reached the place where the fight had occurred the night before, it was daylight, and they had no trouble finding the body of Charlie Frazee. He had been shot once in the chest.

As they rode the fence line toward where they had left the cowboys and the herd, Audie Paget came riding toward them.

"Hey," said Audie, "we found one of them."

"One of what?" asked Happy.

"One of the bastards that attacked us last night," said Audie.

"Dead?" asked Slocum.

"Can't get no deader."

"Where is he?" asked Happy.

"Follow me."

Audie led the way to a place near the fence farther along toward the eastern mountains. A man's body lay on its face. There was an exit wound in his back. Slocum dismounted and walked over to the body. With the toe of his boot, he rolled it over.

"By God," he said. "That's another member of my welcoming committee."

"That's Simon Hemp," said Audie.

"You mean one of the men with Harley Church who beat you up on the road?" asked Joy.

"That's what I mean," said Slocum.

"That's our proof, ain't it?" said Happy. "We know he worked for Fuller. He rode with Church. That's all we need. We got our proof."

Slocum moved back to his horse's side and swung up into the saddle.

"I'm going into town and get the sheriff," he said.

10

Slocum found William Street in the sheriff's office, sitting behind his big desk. When Slocum stepped in, slamming the door behind himself, Street looked up from his paperwork. Slocum wondered just what the hell a sheriff had to write so much about, anyway.

"Well, Slocum," said Street. "What brings you all the way into town?"

"Killings," said Slocum.

Street's face suddenly became grim. He dropped his pen on the desk, leaned back in his chair, and looked straight at Slocum.

"Who's been killed?" he asked.

"Charlie Frazee and a man named Hemp. Maybe a couple more. I ain't sure."

"Simon Hemp?"

"That's what they called him."

"And Charlie Frazee?"

"Yeah."

"That's one from each side," said Street.

"That's right."

"When?" asked Street.

"Last night."

"How'd it happen?"

"A bunch of men attacked the cowboys that was watching our herd last night," said Slocum. "It was getting dark, and we couldn't see them very well, but we shot back. They dropped Charlie, and we dropped at least a couple of them. I figure they picked theirs up in the dark so we wouldn't know who it was we was fighting, but they must have missed Hemp."

"How can you be sure there was any more killed?" asked Street.

" 'Cause I killed one of them," said Slocum. "I know where I was, and I know where he fell. We couldn't find him later on. While the fight was on, the cattle started to run, so it was quite a spell before we could do any looking around. By then it was too dark to see much of anything. We found the two bodies this morning."

Street got up and reached for his gun belt, which he began strapping on.

"Hemp was one of those who jumped me on the road," said Slocum. "I recognized him, and he's known to work for Jim Fuller and ride with Church. This time we got proof of who attacked."

Street reached for his hat.

"Let's go," he said.

Once they reached the scene of the fight, it didn't take the sheriff long to look things over. He saw the two bodies, saw the evidence of the stampede. He talked to Kramer and to all of the cowboys who had been involved in the fight, and he had someone bring him the Fuller Ranch horse that had been picked up running loose on the Kramer Ranch the night before. Then, insisting that Slocum, Happy, and all the rest remain behind, he headed for the Fuller Ranch.

"The damn fool's just going to get himself killed," said Happy. "We'd ought to follow along."

"He told us to stay out of it," said Slocum, "so let's stay."

Bill Street led a horse with a Fuller brand. Slung across the saddle was the body of Simon Hemp. He rode slow and easy onto the Fuller Ranch through the main gate. No one rode to meet him, and he continued toward the big house. As he drew near, Harley Church appeared, but before Church could say or do anything, Fuller himself stepped out onto the porch. The two men waited in silence for Street to stop his horse and start the conversation. The sheriff dropped the reins of the Fuller horse into the dirt.

"This is your horse," he said to Fuller.

"Who's that on him?" asked Fuller.

"You don't know?"

"If I did," said Fuller, "I wouldn't have asked."

Church twisted his head to get a better look.

"That's old Simon," he said. "Simon Hemp."

"Where'd you find him?" asked Fuller.

"He was killed last night when he and some others attacked some Kramer hands over on Kramer's north range. They killed Charlie Frazee and started a stampede. What do you know about it?"

"I don't know anything about it," said Fuller, "and I'm getting damn sick and tired of being accused of every unlawful act that takes place around these parts."

"Jim," said Street, "in the past you've told me that Happy Kramer ran off his own cattle and cut his own fence just to make it look like you done it, and I didn't have any proof against you. But this is different. Two men have been killed. Kramer was attacked last night. There's no doubt about it. One of the attackers was killed, and I've got his body here. He's on one of your horses, and he worked for you."

"I fired him a week ago," said Church. "And when he left, he stole that horse. I figured he'd left the country."

Street shot a look at Fuller.

"That right, Jim?" he asked.

"Harley's my foreman," said Fuller. "If he says he fired the man, then he fired him. I don't watch over his shoulder. I let him run things."

"Well, maybe you ought to keep a closer eye on what's going on, on your own spread," said Street.

"Now just what's that supposed to mean?"

"Never mind. Here's your stolen horse. Don't ever say I ain't doing my job. I'll leave Hemp here for you to deal with, too."

"He ain't our responsibility," said Church. "I told you, I fired him."

"That's all right, Harley," said Fuller. "We'll take care of it. Anything else, sheriff?"

"No," said Street. "Hell. I guess not."

The sheriff's report made Happy furious. He cursed and danced around in circles, stamping his feet.

"What the hell did you expect them to say?" he roared. "Did you expect the bastards to admit it? How much proof does you need? What the hell do you want, anyway? My dead body?"

"Happy," said Street, "I don't like this any more than you do, but if I was to take Jim Fuller to trial on this evidence, he'd walk away from it a free man. Church says that he fired Hemp a week ago, and Hemp stole the horse when he left the ranch. We got no proof to the contrary, and I bet that every man on the Fuller Ranch will back up that story."

"The sheriff's right, Happy," said Slocum. "Calm down before you hurt yourself."

"Well, God damn it to hell," said Happy.

"Sheriff," said Slocum, "can I have a little private talk with you?"

They walked a distance away from the others to gain some privacy. Slocum pulled a cigar out of his pocket and offered one to Street.

"Thanks," said the sheriff. "I believe I will."

Slocum scratched a match on a fence post and lit both smokes.

"I didn't want to ask you in front of Happy," said Slocum, "because he's so damn stubborn about this business. But would you mind telling me, just between the two of us, would you mind telling me what you think? Forget about the proof or no proof or any of that shit. Just tell me what you think."

Street puffed his cigar and looked out across the field. Then he looked back at Slocum.

"I don't know what the hell's going on here, Slocum," he said. "I'm every bit as frustrated as Happy is. I may not be losing any money on this deal, but I'm sure as hell being made to look a fool, and I'd like to find out who it is making me look that way.

"You know, I've known both of those men for a long time. Always liked them both. You want to know what I think? I'll tell you one thing. I don't believe for a minute that Jim Fuller is behind all this rustling and now this killing. If Fuller's men attacked you last night, then I believe that Harley Church was behind it."

"Without the knowledge of his boss?" asked Slocum.

"You asked me what I think," said Street.

"I hadn't thought of that possibility," said Slocum, "but you could be right. Church could be using his job as foreman as a cover for a rustling operation. Do you think that Fuller's that easy to fool, though?''

"He's just like Happy," said Street. "He's so blind
damn mad that he can't see a pile of fresh cow shit
in his path at high noon.''

"Yeah," said Slocum. "I know what you mean.
And I think I know what I need to do.''

"You want to tell me about it?''

"I think it might be better if I didn't do that, sheriff,'' said Slocum, "if you don't mind.''

What Bill Street had said made sense to Slocum. He
had never met Jim Fuller, but Happy and Fuller had
been good friends once. Street liked Fuller and so did
Forrest Harper. And if Fuller was like Happy, as
Street had said, then Slocum could easily see how
Fuller would be "blind damn mad" and not notice
things going on around him. He would be more than
ready to blame anything on Happy, just as Happy was
blaming him.

On the other hand, Slocum had met Church. And
he knew the type. A sinister, cold-blooded bastard
who would do anything to line his own pockets. A
man who enjoyed hurting people. Who would rather
steal money than earn it. It was easy to believe that
Church had taken the job as Fuller's foreman intend-
ing to use it as a front for a rustling operation.

And Fuller had claimed to have lost cattle, too. So
had Harper. If they were telling the truth, and Slocum
couldn't imagine why both men would be lying about

that, then it made even more sense to think that the rustler was Church.

Slocum felt like he had made some progress. He had the whole thing figured out. Really, Street had figured it out for him. But the problem remained the same. There was no proof. The stolen cattle seemed to have disappeared. Unless Church could actually be caught in the act of rustling or be caught with the stolen cattle, no charges could be made against him that would stick.

He hated to admit it, but Slocum could understand the position the sheriff was in. He found himself sympathizing with the lawman, and it was not a feeling that he liked. The sheriff knew, or thought he knew, what was going on, but there was nothing he could do about it.

Well, there was something Slocum could do about it. And he had a double reason for doing it. He still owed Church and one other man for the beating he had suffered at their hands. He had been content to pound up Harve and Red and would have been content to do the same with all the others, perhaps even Church. Conley had forced his hand, and that was okay.

But now, with the almost certain knowledge that Church was behind all the trouble, Slocum decided that he would have to kill Church. He would have his revenge on the man, and Happy's trouble would be over. That was the solution to the problem. Kill Harley Church.

11

"I don't like it, Harley," said Jim Fuller. "Now there's been killing. Did you really fire Simon?"

"What difference does it make, Mr. Fuller?" said Church. "If I hadn't said what I did, you'd be in jail right now. Old Street's tied up with Kramer. That's obvious, ain't it?"

"But they said that you attacked Kramer's men on Kramer property. Is that true?"

"Sure, but only after they killed Sloan and Runt out on the road. They done the first killing. I couldn't let them get away with that. Mr. Fuller, pardon me for saying it, but you're just almost too nice a guy for this business. Old Kramer's been running all over you. Why, I bet he's been stealing your cattle for years. You ever come up short on your count at roundup time? I mean before.''

"Well, yes, but—''

"You see? Ain't no reason for coming up short unless someone's rustling.'' Harley Church picked at the messy scab on his right ear. "But don't you worry about a thing, Mr. Fuller. I'll take care of this little problem.''

Slocum knew what he wanted to do, but he didn't want to carry the fight onto Fuller's land. Alone, he would be foolish to do so, and he didn't want to get the cowboys involved in a range war if he could avoid it. He wasn't sure how many of the Fuller hands were part of Church's gang. He knew only about the six, and he had already cut that number down to two. Church and one other. He didn't know the other's name, but he would recognize him if he saw him again.

The big question was, were those six the whole gang? He had a feeling that once he got Church, the trouble would be over. Oh, there would be some patching up of bad feelings between Happy and Fuller, but once it had been explained to them that Church had been behind all the trouble, they would likely become fast friends again.

So how to get Church without just riding onto the Fuller Ranch after him? Hide and watch. That was the way. But in this gently rolling grassland, there were damn few places to hide. Slocum rode over to where Happy was riding herd.

"Happy," he said, "if you don't see me around for a while, don't worry. I've got some things to do."

"Where you going, Slocum?" said Happy.

"You don't want to know, Happy," said Slocum. "I ain't running out on you, and that's all you need to know."

He touched the brim of his hat, turned his big Appaloosa, and headed west. Soon he had reached the road that led into Dog Leg Creek, and he turned toward the town. The grove of trees from which he had been ambushed was one of the few hiding places around. For that reason, it had already been overused, but he couldn't think of anything else. It provided good concealment with quick access to the road, and everyone from Fuller's, Harper's, and Happy's ranches had to ride that road into town. Everyone passed by that grove sooner or later. He reached the grove and rode into it to wait.

It turned out to be a long and boring day. Three cowboys rode by. He didn't know them. They could have been from either Harper's or Fuller's. But that was all right. He knew that this was going to be a waiting game, and could take some time. He might wind up spending several days like this. But eventually Church would come riding down that road. He would have to. Slocum just hoped that when that time came, Church would be alone.

When the sun got low in the western sky, Slocum decided that his first day of watching from the grove had come to an end. He was hungry, and he wanted a drink. He fired up a cigar and climbed into his saddle, but when he reached the road, he decided to go into Dog Leg Creek instead of back to the ranch. He wasn't sure why. It was a whim.

The town wasn't exactly jumping. In fact, it looked to Slocum like it was just about ready to go to sleep. But there was a café still open, and, of course, the saloon would be doing business for at least a couple more hours. A few horses stood patiently at the hitching rail out front. No noise came out through the batwing doors. Just a handful of quiet drinkers, Slocum thought.

He stopped at the café and had himself a steak dinner washed down with several cups of coffee. It wasn't nearly as good as what Joy fixed up out at the ranch, and it was priced too high. He paid for it and walked over to the saloon.

He had been right. One table was occupied by four local merchants. A couple of cowboys stood at the far end of the bar. That was about it. Slocum walked to the bar and put down a coin. Burl turned to face him.

"Whiskey," said Slocum.

"Yes sir."

Burl put a glass and a bottle in front of Slocum and poured the glass full. He took Slocum's money and went for some change.

"Keep it," said Slocum. "I'll drink it up."

Burl left the bottle.

"I heard you had some trouble out at Happy Kramer's place last night," he said.

"Word travels fast," said Slocum.

"Ain't much to do around here but talk," said Burl. "Work and talk. Work and talk."

Slocum downed his drink and poured himself another one.

"They say Charlie Frazee bought the farm," said Burl.

"That's right."

"Too bad," said Burl. "He was a nice boy."

"What about the ones that bought it on the other side?" Slocum asked. "Were they nice boys?"

Burl shook his head.

"I didn't really know them," he said. "They hadn't been around here very long. They hung out with Harley Church. That's about all I know. They always acted a bit surly, I thought. But Charlie . . ." He shook his head again, slowly. ". . . That's too bad."

The batwings crashed back against the walls, and Slocum glanced over his shoulder to see who was coming in. His eyes narrowed, and he tipped up his glass to finish his whiskey. The cowboy at the door looked at him, hesitated, then stepped on into the room.

"I just came for a drink," said the cowboy. "That's all."

"Yeah," said Slocum, "and I just came for a job, but you and five others jumped me in the road. I think

I've still got a bruise on my ribs from your boot.''

"I ain't looking for a fight.''

"No,'' said Slocum. "I reckon you ain't. Your kind never does, unless he's got plenty of company. You're a yellow-bellied chickenshit.''

The cowboy pulled out his revolver and fired a wild shot. The slug buried itself in the far wall. Slocum drew his Colt and fired. The cowboy screamed as lead tore into his left shoulder. In pain and terror, he lifted his revolver to fire again, but before he could thumb back the hammer, Slocum sent a slug into his chest. He stood swaying for a moment, then fell back, landing with a thud on the hardwood floor. Slocum holstered his Colt, turned back to the bar, and poured himself another whiskey.

"I reckon Bill Street'll be here in a minute,'' he said.

Burl, his eyes wide, nodded his head.

"Yeah,'' he said. "I reckon.''

In just about a minute, Street stepped in the door, gun in hand. He saw the body at once, then he saw Slocum at the bar. He walked over close to Slocum.

"Slocum,'' he said, "you do this?''

"Yeah.''

"The cowboy shot first,'' said Burl. "Slocum here shot in self-defense.''

Street looked toward the merchants still sitting at their table.

"That's right,'' said one, nodding his head. "I seen it.''

"It was like Burl said," added another.

"Slocum," said Street, "I told you, I don't want this fight coming into town."

"I know that," said Slocum, "and I didn't bring it here. I promised you I wouldn't be the one to start anything in town, and I ain't broke that promise. I did call the man a chickenshit. He was one of them that stomped me."

"Damn it, Slocum," said Street, "you provoked him."

"Him and five others stomped all over me," said Slocum, "and all I did was call him a name. I don't consider that provoking on my part. Here. Let me buy you a drink."

"Damn," said Street. "Go ahead. I can use one."

When Slocum stepped inside the Kramer ranch house, the living room was dark. He could see a light on in the kitchen, so he walked over to the door and looked in. There was Joy standing at the cabinet. She had a towel in her hand and was wiping down the cabinet top. She looked over her shoulder at Slocum standing in the doorway, and she smiled.

"Hi," she said.

Slocum unbuckled his gun belt and, carrying it in his right hand, walked on over to stand behind her. He put his gun belt on the cabinet and his arms around her, hugging her close. She leaned back against him, and he kissed her ear.

"Where's Happy?" he asked.

"He's gone to bed," she said. "You have a busy day?"

"A long one. That's all."

She arched her back to press her buttocks against his crotch, and she felt a rising there.

"Oh," she said, "I wondered when this was going to happen again."

"We've been pretty busy," said Slocum.

She reached down to unfasten her jeans, and Slocum stepped back to give her room. He watched as she shoved the jeans down slowly to reveal her marvelous round butt, and he wondered what she was going to do. Was she going to strip right there in the kitchen? Then what? Lie on the table? The floor?

She shoved the jeans down to her knees, and then she leaned forward, her elbows on the counter top. She looked back over her shoulder with a suggestive smile.

"So that's it," said Slocum, and he undid his own britches and dropped them, freeing his swollen cock, which stood out, ready to do service. He moved in close to her, right up against the smooth ass that shined at him in the lantern light.

Gripping his greedy cock, he shoved it in under the lovely cheeks of her ass. She mewed with surprised delight as he rubbed the head around, searching for a place to put it. She arched her back more, thrusting her behind at him, and then he felt the dampness of her juicy cunt. He got the head inside, and she shivered. He thrust forward, and she gasped. He shoved again, and he was deep inside her, and she moaned with pleasure.

"Oh, that's good," she said, and she wiggled her ass from side to side.

Slocum pulled back slowly until he was in danger of slipping out of her tunnel.

"Oh. Oh," she cried.

Then he drove forward, hitting her ass with his pelvis with a loud smack, shoving his hard cock deep into her wonderful, tight wetness. He did the same thing again, and again, and then faster and faster, until he thought that he would explode, but it was too soon for that.

Suddenly, on the upthrust, he stopped. His cock was buried in her, and he held still, pressed hard against her butt. He held her hips tight in his hands as she wiggled her ass for a moment. Then she, too, held still, and Slocum felt the walls of her cunt begin to squeeze, as if milking his cock.

He tried to stay still. He wanted to make it last even longer, but the pressure was intense. The pleasure was very near agony. He pulled back and started to drive again, hard and fast. Joy forced a hand between her own thighs and gripped his balls. The sudden sensation shocked him, and he knew that the gush was coming.

He raised a hand and gave Joy a hard slap on her lovely ass cheek.

"Ah!" she yelled, and he began to spurt, and they came together.

After a moment of profound silence, Slocum slipped out of her. She picked up a towel from the cabinet and wiped him dry. As he was pulling up his trousers, she cleaned herself a bit with the same towel, then pulled her jeans up and fastened them. He stepped up close to her and put his arms around her, and for the first time that evening, they kissed.

Pulling back, Slocum looked deep into her eyes and smiled.

"I hope you didn't wake Happy with that yell," he said.

"If I did," she said, "it was your fault, you bastard. You slapped me."

"Are you mad?"

"No."

She kissed him again, a deep kiss, probing with her tongue.

"I don't think anything could wake Happy tonight," she said. "He was at least half drunk before he went to bed. Why, I bet I could even slip into your room for the night, and he'd never know."

"Well," said Slocum, "why don't we give it a try?"

12

Harley Church was almost in a panic. Things were looking bad. Harve and Red were out of commission, not worth a shit since Slocum broke their bones. Simon Hemp was dead. A couple of days ago, some of the Fuller hands riding the far western reaches of the ranch had come across the body of Conley, all puffed and stinky. And Church's last hand-picked man had been killed by Slocum in the saloon. The witnesses had all called it self-defense.

Church could get the regular cowboys to fight, when they thought the ranch was being threatened, but he couldn't get them to go on raids with him, and none of them wanted to face Slocum. And just that morning, Red and Harve had come to him to tell him that they were cutting out.

"We're getting picked off one at a time," said Red, "and now you and me and Harve here, we're the only ones left. I can't hardly even lift either one of my arms yet, much less handle a gun. And old Harve, well, I guess he could shoot, but he's crying still about how bad his jaws hurt. Right now, we ain't no good in a fight, and we sure don't want to get caught in one neither, the shape we're in."

"All right, all right," Church had said. "Go on and run out on me. Go see the boss. He'll pay you off. Then get the hell out of here. I don't never want to see neither one of you cowardly shits again."

"Well, hell, Harley," said Red, "that ain't no way to be. We'd stay and fight with you if we was healthy. We'd even hang around this place to get healed up, if you had some more men. But the way it is, it just ain't safe. You can see that."

"Aw, go on then," said Church.

And they had, and he was left, for all practical purposes, alone. That Slocum was just too damn good. The man was downright dangerous. Who would ever have counted on anyone like that showing up in the valley? And working for Kramer? Church cursed himself for not having killed Slocum that first day. But how could he have known? Slocum had looked like hell, a beat up, worn out, tired old saddle tramp.

Church had a pretty good thing going in the valley, and he hated to think about losing it. It had been better, though, when he'd had his five gunnies to back up his every play. Still, he did not want to let it go.

Not if he could help it. And he had another, more personal reason to add to everything else. Slocum had damn near shot off his ear. It had hurt, and it was scabby and ugly, and Church was always picking at it. Sometimes he picked at it so much that he made it bleed again.

He had been with a whore in Dog Leg Creek just the other night, and the sight of his puffy, scabby ear, a piece of it dangling loose, had turned her off. She had tried, because she wanted her money, but he could tell, so he had slapped her around a little and then left, furious and unsatisfied.

He hated Slocum, but he was also afraid of Slocum. He needed more gunfighters. He watched as Harve and Red left the big ranch house, mounted up, and rode off toward the road. Good riddance to them, he thought. God damned cowardly bastards. Then he went to the house to see Jim Fuller himself.

"What is it, Harley?" said Fuller.

"That was my last two men that just quit," said Church. "Did you know that?"

"Yes," said Fuller, "I know. I paid them off in full."

"I can't operate short-handed like this," said Church. "I need to hire some more."

"I don't see any need for it," said Fuller. "I wondered when I first hired you why you needed to bring five men with you. I thought I had need of your—special services—so I didn't argue, but I've got a full crew of ranch hands. That's all we need."

"Not with all this fighting going on, it ain't," said Church. "Them cowboys of yours ain't gunfighters. Hell. We need some men who are paid to fight, who fight and kill for a living. Know how to handle themselves in a tough situation. That Slocum's a bad one, and it ain't going to be easy to get rid of him. It's going to take some special men with special talents and guts to face that son of a bitch."

"I didn't hire you to get rid of anybody, Harley," said Fuller. "I'm not a murderer. I hired you to stop rustlers from getting my cattle. That's all, and it seems to me that things have gotten way out of hand. I want it to stop before it gets any worse."

"Well, hell, it's going to get worse, no matter what you do. If you're smart, you'll be ready for it when it happens."

"It's not going to get any worse because of anything I do," said Fuller, "or because of anything you do while you're in my employ."

"You ain't going to let me hire on new hands?"

"No, I'm not."

"Then by God you can start defending yourself against Kramer's hired guns," said Church. "If I can't bring in more men to help me in this, then I quit. You hear me? God damn it, I quit. And when they've drove off your last cow, and maybe shot you dead to boot, then you'll be sorry, by God, and you'll wish you'd listened to me when you had the chance."

"Have it your own way, Harley," said Fuller, and Church turned and stomped out of the house, slamming the door behind him. Fuller poured himself a drink, wondering if he had done the right thing by letting Church go. Then he wondered if he had made a mistake by hiring the man in the first place. The whole situation was very confusing. It had been, ever since he and Happy Kramer, old friends, had their initial falling out.

It was branding time, and Slocum was at the corral watching when he noticed a rider, a young boy, galloping his horse up the lane toward the ranch house. He turned to watch, wondering who the young fellow was and what he was up to. He saw the boy pull his horse to a stop by the porch, and watched as Joy stepped out onto the porch to talk with the lad. He saw the boy hand a piece of paper to Joy, then turn and ride back down the lane toward the road, not nearly in as big a hurry going as he had been coming. Joy looked at the paper she held for a moment, then stepped off the porch and started toward the corral. Slocum walked to meet her.

"John," she said, "this came for you from Harley Church. That boy said Harley gave him fifty cents to bring it out here."

Curious, Slocum took the paper from Joy and unfolded it to read the message. The handwriting was painfully laborious.

Slokam,
You bastard. Lets have it out you and me man to

man just the to of us. I aint skeered of you anyway
and unles your skeered of me youll meat me on
top of the rimroks north of dawg leg crick tomorra
morning at first lite. One of us will git kild.

Yrs turly,
Harley J. Church

ps lets git this thang seddled bitween us onse and
for all.   HJC

Joy watched Slocum's face as he read.

"You're not thinking of going to meet him, are you?" she asked.

"Hell, yes, I'm going," said Slocum. "This is just the chance I been looking for. Besides, the little shit spelled my name wrong."

"Be serious, John."

"I am. If I can get rid of Harley Church, all your rustling troubles'll be over with. Old Bill Street even told me that he didn't believe that Mr. Fuller had anything to do with any rustling. He said he thought that it was all Church's doing. Well, I ain't said anything to Happy about it, but I agree with old Street on that. Church and his gang have been causing all this trouble all along. And I think his gang's all wiped out. That leaves just him, and this is my chance to finish him off."

"But what about all that proof that everyone was so God damned worried about?" said Joy.

"If the rustlers are all dead," said Slocum, "then

who the hell cares about the proof anymore? The problem's solved.''

"John," she said, "it's bound to be a trap. Do you actually believe that Harley Church will just stand up there in plain view, waiting to engage in a fair fight with you?''

"No," said Slocum, "I don't. I ain't that stupid. So I'll be ready for his trap.''

"But John—"

"Joy, I'm going to meet him up there in the morning, and that's all there is to it.''

Joy stamped her foot.

"Shit," she said, and she turned to stomp her way back to the house and up onto the porch. Then she went inside, slamming the door so hard that Slocum was sure she must have broken something.

Slocum was up in the middle of the night. He packed some food and a bottle of whiskey. He made sure he had several good cigars and some sulphur matches in a tin. He checked his Colt and his Winchester and packed a couple of extra boxes of shells. He strapped on his six-gun, put on his hat, shouldered his saddle-bags, took his rifle in hand, and slipped out of the house as quietly as he could.

He saddled up the Appaloosa in the corral, put the rifle in the saddle boot, and mounted up. It was a good long ride to the rimrocks, and he wanted to be there well before sunup. He knew Church's plan. At the bottom of the rimrocks, the road turned west, then wound its way up on top and turned east again.

A man just riding up to the top as the sun was coming up would find himself blinded by the early-morning sunlight. To the east, there were several large outcroppings of boulders, and it was somewhere there that Harley Church would be hidden, waiting with a rifle for Slocum to top the rise facing into the sun. Well, it wasn't going to happen that way.

He took his time riding. There was no hurry, really, and he did not want to take a chance on his horse hurting himself by a misstep in the dark. He went down the road past the gate to the Harper Ranch and on past the sinister grove of trees. He rode past the town of Dog Leg Creek, then through the creek, and he turned to start climbing to the top of the rimrocks.

It was time to be careful. Church was likely already in his hiding place, but he would probably not be expecting Slocum until sunup. Still, Slocum did not want to call attention to himself by making any unnecessary noise. He turned his mount to the north, riding off the road, and he made the straightest line he could to the nearest boulders.

The outcropping ran more or less southeast, and if Slocum had Church figured out right, the bush-whacker would be farther on down toward the southeast end near the edge of the rimrocks, where the sun would rise right behind him.

Slocum reached the rocks and dismounted. He led the horse around behind some boulders and tied him there. Then he pulled off the saddle. He ate some hard biscuits and took a slug of whiskey. Then he shouldered his saddlebags and took up his Winchester and started making his way on foot through the boulders in a southeasterly direction. He wanted to get closer to Church, but not too close.

He moved slowly to avoid slipping on the rocks or stepping into a hole. The footing was unsure at best. In the dark it could be treacherous. When he estimated that he had made it about halfway from where he had left his horse to the edge of the rimrocks, he stopped. This would be close enough, at least for now. He looked around a little, until he found a relatively smooth spot, and then he settled down to get a little sleep and to wait for the sun to make its early-morning appearance.

13

Happy Kramer, Joy, and Audie Paget rode into Dog Leg Creek early the next morning. Happy had left Sully Nolan, his foreman, in charge at the ranch. They rode straight to the office of William Street and barged in on the sheriff.

"Bill," said Happy, his voice demanding, "you've got to do something."

"Whoa," said Street. "How about a good morning at least?"

"Good morning, Bill," said Happy. "You've got to do something."

"Good morning, Happy," said Street. "Miss Kramer, Audie."

"Good morning, sheriff," said Joy.

Audie mumbled and touched the brim of his hat.

"Now, Happy," said Street, "what have I got to do something about?"

"Slocum's gone off to kill Church," said Happy. "Or more likely, get himself killed. It'll be an ambush. It'll be murder. That's what it'll be."

"Shut up, Happy," said the sheriff. "Go over there and sit down."

He indicated a chair against the far wall. Happy gave Street a withering look of rage, but he slumped his way over to the chair and sat. Street watched him for a moment, then turned to Joy and Audie.

"Now," he said, "can either one of you tell me what this is all about?"

"Yes," said Joy. "Yesterday evening the Johnson boy came riding out to the ranch with a note from Harley Church. He said that Church gave him fifty cents to deliver it. I took the note and read it. It was addressed to John Slocum, and it challenged him to meet Church on top of the rimrocks this morning at first light. John left some time in the middle of the night. I know he's gone up there to meet Church."

"There's going to be a killing for sure," said Happy.

"Well," said Street, "let's ride up there and see what we can see. Miss Joy, you can wait for us here in my office if you like."

"Like hell," said Joy. "I'm riding along."

Slocum had been awake to see the first light of the sun peek over the far eastern horizon. He eased himself to the edge of a big boulder to have a look around. He saw no sign of Harley Church. He hadn't really expected to. He figured that Church, like Slocum himself, was snugged down behind some boulders somewhere, waiting to shoot from his hiding place.

But two could play a waiting game, and Slocum figured that Church was probably not a man of much patience. It wouldn't take long for him to decide that Slocum wasn't coming, had not accepted his challenge. Then he would come crawling out of his rocks and show himself.

The sun was completely up when Church at last did what Slocum had expected him to do. He crept out at first, then stood up in plain view to get a look around. He was maybe two hundred yards away. Slocum came out of his nook and stood on top of a boulder. He called out in a strong voice.

"Looking for me?"

Church turned quickly, spotted Slocum, and jerked off a shot from his rifle. It was wide. Slocum raised his Winchester to his shoulder and took aim, but Church dropped down behind a boulder just as Slocum squeezed off his shot.

"Damn," said Slocum, dropping down behind the rocks. He decided to shorten the distance between him and Church, and he started to work his way around and between the big boulders, careful to stay down behind them at the same time. Now each man knew the other was there. It would be a hunt to the death.

He had moved toward Church about as far as he dared. There was a possibility at least that Church was doing the same thing as was he, so they could be pretty close to each other. Slocum crouched, waited, and listened. He heard no sign of movement in the rocks. He told himself, somebody's going to have to do something sooner or later.

Carefully, he crawled out of his hole and up on top of a big boulder. He was flat on his belly, his Winchester in his right hand. He raised his head to look around, and he saw nothing. Where is the little shit? he asked himself. Then, to find out, he stood up.

From his hiding place, his rifle barrel laid out over the top of a rock, Church took aim and fired. The bullet took the heel off Slocum's right boot. He yowled as he lost his footing, coming down hard on his backside on top of the big boulder and sliding forward. His Winchester clattered down the other side of the rock.

Slocum at last stopped sliding when he crashed into a tight crevice and found himself wedged in. He heard a whoop of delight and victory from Church, who, having seen the fall, must have thought that he had hit more than a boot heel. Church would be making his way over to inspect the damages, and Slocum had lost his Winchester.

He thought that he could work his way out from between the rocks with a little time, but if he tried it,

Church might come upon him. He couldn't afford to let down his guard long enough to try to free himself. He reached for his Colt, but there was almost no space between the rock and his waist, and the gun handle was just beyond his reach.

He had to have it. He flattened his palm against his side and shoved downward. His fingers were squeezed in tight. He pushed harder, gritting his teeth against the pain as he felt the skin on the back of his hand being flayed. His fingertips touched the handle of the Colt.

Then he realized there was no way he would get the hand back out, not wrapped around the handle of the revolver. He heard the crunch of footsteps on the boulders, and he could tell that they were coming nearer. He'd be shot like a fish in a trap. What a hell of a way to go. Well, he thought, I guess one way's no better than another, but he hated for the last thing he saw on this earth to be the grinning face of Harley Church.

"Slocum?" he heard Church say. "Slocum, you still alive? Did I get you, boy? Where are you, Slocum?"

The voice was very near. Then the footsteps sounded again, but slowly, one careful step at a time. Slocum looked up from his trap. There was no way he could hide. As soon as Church came on top of the big boulder above, the one from which Slocum had fallen, he would look down and see Slocum there in plain view.

He heard another footstep. His hand would not come out the way it had gone in. The pressure of the rocks holding him was bruising his ribs. It was a tight squeeze, but he wondered if he could manage to turn somehow, to twist his body to a new position where maybe the hand would come out. He tried, tentatively. He couldn't move.

It would have to be done all at once, with one mighty effort, a violent, fast, wrenching turn. He took a deep breath, feeling the pressure on his ribs, and he spun his shoulders with all his strength. He yelled from the effort and the pain, and he looked up just in time to see Church look over the edge of the boulder, and at the same time, his gun hand came up clutching the Colt, and he fired.

He fired fast, and he saw some blood fly and heard Church's scream. Then he could hear the sounds of Church's feet as the bad man scampered away. The sounds soon faded, and Slocum could only figure that he had wounded Church, and Church had fled.

Slocum struggled, trying to free himself, but when he had twisted to free up his gun hand, he had also fallen deeper into the crack. A grim image came into his mind of someone someday walking over the boulders and looking down into the pit to see his bleached bones, the skull grinning back at them. "I wonder who that was," they would say.

He was just about to give up all hope, when he heard someone call his name. He listened. Again he heard it. A man calling his name. It wasn't Church.

He could tell that much. But who would it be? Then there was a different voice, and it did not call his last name.

"John. John," it called. "Are you out here?"

It was Joy. He would know her voice anywhere and under any circumstances. He lifted his head and drew in as much air as he could.

"Up here," he shouted. "In the rocks."

The voices called out to him again, and again he answered, until by following the sounds, Joy, Happy, Audie, and Bill Street looked down on him from the big boulder above.

"Can you get out of there?" asked Street.

"I'm stuck fast."

"Hang on," said Happy. "I'll get a rope."

Happy disappeared from Slocum's vision.

"Where's Church?" asked Street.

"He took off," said Slocum. "At least I think he did. I winged him from down here."

"How'd you get down there, anyway?" asked Audie.

"Bastard shot my boot heel off, and I fell."

"John," said Joy, "are you hurt?"

"Just bruised and scraped up," said Slocum. "I'll be all right if I can ever get out of here."

"Just hang on, old pard," said Audie. "Happy's coming with a rope."

When Happy returned, he payed out a loop and dropped it over Slocum. Slocum raised his arms, one at a time, so as not to slip farther into the trap, and

Happy drew the loop in until it was under Slocum's arms and around his chest.

"You ready?" asked Happy.

Slocum gripped the rope with his left hand. He still held the Colt in his bloody right hand.

"Haul away," he said.

Happy, Audie, and Street pulled on the rope, and Slocum felt himself raised a bit. They braced themselves and pulled again, and Slocum was able to holster the Colt and grab the rope with both hands. Joy grabbed onto the end of the rope to give a hand to the other three, and they pulled again. This time Slocum came free. He was able to get a foot out of the hole and onto solid rock. From there, holding the rope, he managed to climb back up onto the big boulder.

"Thanks," he said. "I thought I was going to starve to death down there."

His shirt was torn and bloody, and the back of his right hand was raw. He started to walk, carefully, toward the rear of the outcropping.

"Where you going?" asked Happy.

"I left my saddlebags back over there," said Slocum. "There's some whiskey in them, and I need a drink."

They followed Slocum back to the spot where he had spent the night, and he dug the whiskey bottle out of his saddlebags. He took a long slug and offered the bottle to Street.

"No, thanks," said the sheriff.

"Give me some of that stuff," said Happy.

"Sure," said Slocum, handing the bottle to Happy. "It's yours, anyhow."

Happy drank and passed the bottle to Audie. Audie drank and gave it back to Slocum, who took one more healthy swallow, then stuffed the bottle back into the saddlebags. He slung the bags over his shoulder and winced with pain as they slapped against his bruised and scraped back. He started to walk.

"Where you going now?" asked Happy.

"I left my horse down this way."

"Well, then," said Happy, "we'll meet you back down there where the road turns to go down to the valley."

"I ain't going down to the valley," said Slocum.

Joy ran after him and got around in front of him to block his path. She stood firm, looking up into his eyes with a hard stare.

"And just where are you going, then?" she asked.

"I'm going after Church," said Slocum. "I aim to finish what I came up here to do."

"He's got too much of a start on you," she said. "You'll never catch him."

"He's hurt," said Slocum. "He'll slow down."

"Damn it, John," she said, "you're hurt yourself. You need some tending to."

"It'll keep," he said.

Joy looked toward her uncle and the other men.

"Happy?"

"I can't stop him," said Happy, "if he's set on going."

Audie gave a shrug.

"Sheriff," said Joy, "are you just going to let him ride off from here like that with the intention of killing a man?"

"There's nothing I can do until someone's done been killed," said Street, "and in this case, I doubt if I'll do anything then. Besides, by the time Slocum catches up with old Church, they'll probably be over the county line."

"Oh, damn it!" said Joy. She stamped her foot and turned back on Slocum. "We should have left you stuck down in that hole, you stubborn jackass."

Slocum reached out with both hands and took her by the shoulders. He pulled her to him and kissed her full on the lips. Happy's eyes opened wide in near disbelief. Slocum released Joy and stepped back, looking into her eyes.

"Don't worry about me," he said. "I'll be all right, and I'll be coming back."

He stepped around her and walked on toward the place where he'd left the Appaloosa waiting several hours before. Street looked at Happy.

"You reckon we'll ever see him again?" he asked.

Happy stared after Slocum for a moment. Then he looked at Joy.

"How long has that been going on?" he asked.

"Since the first day he rode in."

Happy sighed.

"Yeah," he said. "I reckon he'll be back."

14

Outside the valley, up on top of the rimrocks and beyond the outcropping of boulders, the land was flat and not so lush as it was below. The heat was more intense, and the air dustier. Slocum recalled how parched he had felt as he had ridden into this country, and how welcome the valley below had seemed, that is, until he met his welcoming committee.

Harley Church's tracks led clearly out onto this wide flat, but Slocum scanned the horizon and saw no sign of Church. Something was wrong somewhere, he thought. The pieces of the puzzle did not fit together. It made sense that Church would want to get rid of Slocum, just as Slocum wanted to get rid of him. And the ambush from the boulders had been well planned, but it had not worked out the way Church had figured it. Church had been hurt and had fled.

Slocum had no real idea how badly Church was hurt. He had fired so fast, and Church had disappeared from his view so quickly that he did not know where he had hit the man. He distinctly remembered seeing blood fly, but the blood caused by a wound could be misleading. He knew that.

Still, Church was hurt. Slocum had hit him. It made no sense for Church to be headed north across this barren land. It was a long haul to the next town, even to any lone ranch or farmhouse. Slocum knew that much from recent experience.

It was a bad enough ride for a man prepared for it and in good health. It would be utterly stupid for Church to try it with a fresh wound, and Slocum had accused Church of all kinds of things, but so far, nothing indicated that he was stupid.

Besides all that, why would Church be lighting out when he had the safety and comfort of the Fuller Ranch down in the valley? Something at the back of Slocum's mind was gnawing at him, telling him that he was being played for a sucker. But how?

The tracks were clear. They led away from the outcropping, straight north, into the vast openness. But Church would have had to travel pretty damn fast to be already clean out of sight. Slocum wasn't that far behind him, and Slocum's eyesight was still as good as most.

Then Church's tracks took a sudden and sharp turn to the left, west, and Slocum followed them for maybe a hundred yards before they turned again to the south. Church was headed back down into the valley, might even already be there. He had ridden off north just long enough to cause Slocum to waste some time and energy following him the wrong way. He might even have hoped that Slocum would lose the trail and keep going north. If Church could manage to get to the Fuller Ranch before Slocum could catch up to him, Slocum thought, then all this effort and all this pain would have been wasted.

He turned the big Appaloosa and headed for the road.

When Slocum reached the main gate of the Fuller Ranch, he had not seen another sign of Church. He figured that Church had beat him back to the ranch and was safe inside, his wounds being tended to. He started to ride on back to Kramer's and tell Joy that she had gotten her wish, and that he had been played for a fool, but then he had another thought, a sudden and perhaps foolish one. He turned and rode through the gate and headed down the lane toward the Fuller ranch house.

As he drew close to the house, an imposing figure of a man standing on the porch spoke to him.

"You'd be Slocum," he said.

"I am," said Slocum.

"I'm Jim Fuller," said the other. "You look like hell, like someone tried to skin you."

"Someone did try," said Slocum. "I followed him back here."

"Not here," said Fuller. "Who do you think you followed here?"

"Your foreman, Harley Church," said Slocum. "The little weasel sent me a note to meet him at first light up on the rimrocks. He laid an ambush up there, but I figured he'd try something like that, so I slipped up early. We traded shots. I hit him once, and he took off. He tried to make me think he was headed north, but he doubled back and came down into the valley."

"You were right behind him?"

"No, I was delayed a bit, but I followed his tracks."

"You didn't follow his tracks back here?"

"Well, no," said Slocum. "Not exactly. I followed them back down off the rim. Then I lost them in the heavy tracks to and from town. I figured he'd come back here though. Where else would he go?"

"I don't know," said Fuller, "but Harley quit me yesterday. He wanted to hire some more gun hands and I refused."

"He quit?"

"That's right. I don't expect you to believe me, the way things have been between me and your boss, but—"

"No," said Slocum. "I believe you."

"You're welcome to look around."

"No, thanks. Bill Street told me that he thought Church was behind all the trouble between you and

Happy, and I tend to feel the same way. If you say he ain't here, I believe you. It's just that the little bastard has suckered me twice now, and I don't like that.''

Slocum went back into Dog Leg Creek and rode the distance of the main street slowly and cautiously. When he passed the sheriff's office, Street stepped out and called his name.

Slocum stopped and looked over his shoulder. Street walked after him.

''What the hell are you doing in town?'' he asked.

''The little bastard turned back,'' said Slocum. ''He's here. Somewhere.''

''Are you sure?''

''I'm sure he turned back,'' said Slocum, ''and he ain't out at Fuller's place. He's hurt. Where else would he be?''

''Damn it,'' said Fuller. ''I'll go over and check at Doc's. Why don't you get the hell back out to the ranch and let me handle this? If he's in town, I'll find him.''

Slocum didn't answer. He sat in his saddle and watched as Street headed for the doctor's office. Then he finished his ride down to the far end of town. The horses at the hitching rails didn't tell him anything. He didn't know what horse Church had been riding. None of the animals he saw looked as if they had just been taken for a hard ride, either.

He turned around and looked back down the street. There weren't too many places in Dog Leg Creek a man like Church could hide, especially when he was hurt. Slocum rode over to the big front door of the livery stable, the last building on the east end of the street. An old man sat in a chair leaning back against the wall.

"Howdy, son," he said, as Slocum approached.

"A man come in here on a hard rode horse?" asked Slocum.

"Ain't nobody come in today," said the old man. "I might just as well have stayed in bed."

"You know Harley Church?"

"Know who he is."

"You seen him today?"

"Nope."

Slocum could see, on down the way, William Street coming back out of the doctor's office. Apparently he had not found Church in there.

"Thanks," he said, and he rode around the east end of the building to the back. About halfway down, he could see a horse tied behind a building. He rode in that direction.

"Ow. God damn it. Be careful," said Harley Church. "That hurts."

Church was sitting on the edge of a bed, his shirt off, and a woman was tying a bandage around the flesh of his upper right arm.

"Well, don't yell at me," she said. "I'm doing the best I can. I told you to go see Doc."

"And I told you I can't go and see Doc," said

Church. "I told you to take care of it."

"I shouldn't do anything for you," she said. "Not after what you done to me the last time you was here."

"Aw, shut up," said Church. "I didn't hurt you none."

"You did, too. You did hurt me."

"You're all right now, ain't you? So what are you bitching about?"

There was a knock on the door, and Church grabbed his revolver. He thumbed back the hammer. The woman gasped.

"Veronica?" came a voice from the other side of the door. "Veronica, you in there?"

"Who is it?" she said.

"Veronica, it's Bill Street. Is anyone in there with you?"

Church shook his head, and Veronica answered.

"No." Her voice was trembling.

"I've got to come in and check the room," said Street. "Will you open the door?"

"No. I—I'm not dressed."

"Veronica, I'm coming in."

They could see the doorknob turning, and Church sprang up off the bed to stand just in front of the door. He fired a shot, then another, through the door, and they heard a groan from the other side, then a thump. Veronica screamed.

"Shut up," snapped Church, as he grabbed his shirt. He jerked the door open, and there was Bill

Street, sitting in the hall, his back against the wall on the other side, his chest covered with blood. His eyes rolled up to look Harley Church in the face, and Church fired another shot into his chest. Then he ran down the hall.

Outside in the alley, Slocum had come to within fifty feet of the tied horse. He wasn't really close enough yet to be sure, but he thought that the poor beast looked like it had been badly used. It could be Church's horse, he thought. It made sense to Slocum that the wounded fugitive would pull up in the alley and sneak in someplace.

But where would he be? Where, under the circumstances, would he manage to find a safe haven for himself? Slocum wasn't really familiar with Dog Leg Creek even yet, and he especially couldn't tell from the back just what buildings he was looking at.

The saloon? The hotel? He drew closer. Yes. The horse was tied behind the hotel. Church must have a friend in there who was willing to hide him and get him some kind of medical attention, Slocum thought, if that was really his horse.

Just then, Slocum heard two gunshots, and then a third. The back door of the hotel flew open, and Harley Church came rushing into the alley, a gun in his right hand. He had a wild and frantic look about him. He was going for the horse, but he saw Slocum. Church sent a quick shot in Slocum's direction, and Slocum flung himself from the saddle to avoid it.

He landed hard, partly against the packed dirt of

the alley, partly against the back wall of the saloon next door to the hotel. He fumbled for his own Colt as Church tried desperately to get control of his horse, which had been spooked by the sudden activity and the gunshot.

Church had managed to get one foot into a stirrup, his left hand on the saddle horn. At the same time, he twisted to fire another shot at Slocum, but Slocum jerked off a quick round. It tore through Church's left hand and buried itself in the saddle horn.

Church screamed in pain. The horse turned and ran down the alley. Church's foot slipped from the stirrup and he fell. Scrambling to his feet, he fired back at Slocum, his bullet crashing into the wall just by Slocum's head. Then he jerked open the back door of the hotel and ran back inside.

Slocum got up to his feet and followed, but when he reached the door, he found that it had been bolted from the inside. He jerked at it a few times, then backed up and crashed into it with his shoulder. The door was heavy and solid.

"Damn," he said, and he turned and ran back to his Appaloosa, waiting patiently for him there where he had dismounted so ingloriously. He got quickly into the saddle and raced the horse back around the end of the stable and out into the main street.

By the time he reached the front of the hotel, people were already crowding around its front door, looking into the windows to try to see what the excitement was all about. As Slocum jumped out of his saddle, he saw Burl, the bartender from next door, a shotgun in his hands, run into the hotel.

"Burl," he shouted. "Watch out."

But Burl was already inside. His Colt in hand and cocked, Slocum ran for the door. Just as he stepped inside, the shotgun roared. Slocum stared, wide-eyed, as Harley Church, on the stairway, leaned back against the wall, the front of his upper torso a mass of bloody flesh, the expression on his face a blank. He slid down the wall slowly, leaving a smear of blood above him, until he wound up in a sitting position. Then he slowly fell sideways, to his own left, and stretched out dead on the stairs.

Slocum stepped up beside Burl.

"The son of a bitch killed Bill Street," said Burl. "That's what they said."

"Oh, no!" said Slocum. "Where is the sheriff?"

From the top of the stairs, a scantily clad, slightly trembling Veronica provided the answer.

"He's up here," she said.

Slocum and Burl walked upstairs together. They found Street, still leaning against the wall, the way Church had left him. Slocum noted the holes in the door across from the body.

"He never had a chance," he said. "The little shit shot him through the door."

"Bill Street was a good man," said Burl.

"Yes," said Slocum. "He was."

He could have said much more, but he didn't bother. Street had been one of the few lawmen Slocum had ever had any real respect for—had even, he admitted now that the man was dead—had even liked. He thought that if he had killed Church up on the rimrocks that morning the way he should have, Street would still be alive.

If—Slocum shook those thoughts from his mind. What was done was done. He knelt down beside the body and gently stretched it out on the floor. Then he stood up again. At least, he thought, the trouble's all over now.

15

The news of the death of Harley Church and the related assumption that the rustling problems had been brought to an end and the feared range war averted was tempered by the simultaneous news of the killing of Sheriff William Street. The man had not only the reputation of a good lawman, but he was also well liked in the town and the valley that it served.

After a long talking to by both Slocum and his niece Joy, Happy Kramer grudgingly admitted that he had likely misjudged his old friend Jim Fuller, and that probably everything had, after all, been instigated by the murderous Harley Church.

Joy suggested a big celebration to be held at the Kramer Ranch to ring in the new era in the valley, and to bring old friends back together, and Happy concurred.

"But we'll have to wait a respectful time after the funeral," he said. "We don't want to be having a big shindig too soon after the unfortunate demise of our friend Bill Street."

Joy agreed. She did suggest, however, that they all ride over to Fuller's for a visit.

"What do you mean, we all?" said Happy.

"Well," she said, "You and me and maybe John."

"And just what the hell are we going to do when we get there?"

"To begin with," said Joy, "you and Mr. Fuller are going to shake hands, and then I'm going to tell him about the plans for our get-together."

"You two don't need me along for that," said Slocum. "It seems to me that's something for old friends, and I'm new around here. I'd just be in the way."

"Nonsense," said Joy.

"Well, you don't need me for it, neither," said Happy.

But Joy insisted, and when she did that, she usually got her way. The three of them rode over to the Fuller Ranch, and Jim Fuller, as was his habit, stepped out onto the porch when he heard them approaching. They pulled up just a few feet away. Happy and Fuller glared at each other.

"Hello, Mr. Fuller," said Joy.

"Hello, Miss Kramer. Slocum."

"Howdy," said Slocum.

"Well, since there's no greeting for me at all," said Happy, "I guess I'll just turn my old horse around go right on back home."

"Happy," said Joy.

"I told you it was a no-good idea for me to come over here," said Happy.

"I'm wondering just what you did come over here for," said Fuller.

"Oh," said Happy, "so he's talking to me now, is he? Did you notice that, you two?"

"Only because you've actually come onto my property after all this time," said Fuller, "after all the names you've called me and after all the times you've threatened to kill me."

"And I suppose you never called me a name," said Happy. "Never threatened my own life?"

"After you started it," shouted Fuller.

"After I started it?" roared Happy. "Everything was all right until you started with the accusations. Calling me a cattle thief and all."

"Oh damn it," said Joy. She looked at Slocum. "I should've listened to Happy in the first place. This was a stupid idea."

"Maybe not," said Slocum. He pulled out his Colt and fired a shot into the air. The suddenness of it startled both Fuller and Happy into stunned silence.

"Would you two quiet down for a minute and let someone else say something?" Slocum asked.

A cowboy with a revolver in his hand came running around the corner of the house.

"Mr. Fuller," he shouted, "are you all right?"

"Yes," said Fuller. "Everything's fine here, Curly. You can go on back to work."

"You sure?"

Curly, ready to shoot, looked suspiciously at the visitors, especially Slocum.

"I'm sure," said Fuller. "Thanks, Curly. It's all right."

Curly hesitated, shoved his gun back into its holster, and turned to walk slowly away, glancing back suspiciously every now and then.

"Okay, Slocum," said Fuller. "You got our attention. Say your piece."

"Well," said Slocum, "to start with, the reason Happy come over here today was to shake your hand. We figure, like poor old Bill Street figured, that the trouble between you two was all caused by Church. You all used to be friends, good friends, I'm told, and there ain't no reason you shouldn't be again. Old Church, he put one over on both of you, but he's gone now, and I think it'd be pretty bullheaded of you to let him have the last laugh—even from the grave."

Happy stared in silence at his saddle horn. Fuller stared at the porch boards between his feet. After no one spoke for a long and awkward moment, Joy broke the silence.

"Well," she said, "what John said's the truth. Hasn't either one of you stubborn jackasses got anything to say?"

"Why don't we all go inside and have a drink of whiskey?" said Fuller.

"That sounds like the smartest idea yet," said Slocum. He dismounted and stepped up onto the porch. Joy followed him. Happy was the slowest of the three to get down off his horse. Looking at the ground the whole time, he shuffled his way up onto the porch to stand in front of Jim Fuller, his old friend and recent enemy. With an obvious effort, he stuck out his hand. Fuller studied it for a brief moment, then reached up to grip it hard.

"Come on in," he said.

Fuller's whiskey was good, and after a few drinks, he and Happy were talking like old friends once again. Both Slocum and Joy began to feel like they were in the way. Then the conversation turned to something they could all take part in.

"There's something that's puzzling me yet," said Fuller. "Harley Church, who I was fool enough to hire, stole cattle from both you and me."

"From Harper, too," said Happy.

"Yeah. From all three of us. But what the hell did he do with them? Where did he take them? How did he manage to get them away from here without anyone ever seeing any sign of where he was going with them?"

"Well," said Happy, scratching his head and scrunching up his face in puzzlement, "there's a lot of open range around here."

"But it's all wide open and flat," said Fuller. "You could see a bunch of cows going off in any direction for a day or two."

"It's not open to the east," said Joy.

"No," said Happy, "but you couldn't drive cows into them mountains. No way."

"Well, Church and all of his boys but two are dead," said Slocum, "and those two have left the country. We'll probably never know what they did with the stolen cattle."

Jim Fuller went after the bottle and poured another round.

"You're probably right about that," he said. "At least it's all over and done."

They had a few more drinks and made plans to attend the funeral of William Street together. Then Joy told Fuller of her planned celebration and invited him and all his cowboys to attend. Fuller accepted the invitation, and soon after that, Slocum, Happy, and Joy took their leave and returned to the Kramer ranch.

Joy had agreed with her uncle that they couldn't have the big celebration too soon after the funeral. She would wait a respectable time, but she could start making plans, and she started by thinking about the menu. They would have plenty of beef, of course. Fuller had already said that he would contribute some, and she expected that Harper would do the same. There would be no shortage of beef with three big ranchers getting together. But she thought that some variety in meats would be appropriate for the party.

Hunting was good in the mountains to the east, and there were plenty of cowboys on the ranch who could shoot and would probably enjoy the change of pace.

Slocum agreed, and since he had no more rustlers to chase and no real idea what his job should be anymore, he decided that he would be the first to go. He packed up for a few days in the mountains: guns, ammunition, camp supplies, food, coffee, whiskey, cigars, and matches. He took his Appaloosa to ride and an extra horse from the ranch for a pack animal. Then he headed east, into the mountains just off the Kramer range.

He saw a few deer his first day out, but they were small, and he let them go. He thought that if he came across a good large buck, he might take it, but he was really interested in elk.

That first night he made a small camp and fixed his own meal. It wasn't at all bad, he thought, being out like that, if one had all the supplies he needed, and as long as he knew that once the supplies started to run low, he had some place nearby to go back to.

It was a little after noon of the second day when he spotted the big elk on a high ridge. It was too far for a good shot, so he began stalking, trying to get closer without frightening it away. The animal moved north along the top of the mountains, apparently unaware of any danger. Slocum followed on the Appaloosa, leading the packhorse.

A couple of hours later, he thought that he had a chance. He slowly brought out his Winchester, took careful aim, and fired. The elk leapt forward, then fell.

"Got him," said Slocum.

Carefully, he marked the spot in his mind. By the time he got up there to it, he knew, it would look different. He had to ride up to the ridge and then a distance north along the top before he would come to the spot where the elk had fallen. He urged the Appaloosa forward, pulling the packhorse behind by a long rope.

It was a steep climb and somewhat treacherous, but they made it to the ridge. Slocum sat still for a moment, surveying the country around from this new, near dizzying height. It was beautiful country, especially the green valley below. He could actually see the ranch houses of Kramer, Fuller, and Harper, and he could even see the town of Dog Leg Creek. It was a magnificent view.

But there was a freshly killed elk ahead, and he wanted to get to it before any opportunistic predators happened along. As he rode ahead, he thought he smelled rain in the air. He decided to get his elk and hurry right back down to the ranch house.

He had ridden the ridge to a point beyond the northern limits of Happy's range. If he were to go straight west down out of the mountains, he would be on the Harper spread. None of the ranch property below, though, as he understood it, extended up into the mountains.

Slocum found his elk, and he field dressed it and loaded it onto the packhorse. He was ready to go back, but he needed a short breather. He pulled the whiskey bottle out of his pack and took a slug. Then he decided to have a smoke and enjoy the scenery for just a little longer.

It was then that he heard the cows. Not a large herd, but a fairly substantial number, were lowing somewhere not too far away. He looked around, surveying the area, and he was sure that he was too far away from Harper's range for Harper's cattle to be making the sounds he was hearing.

"What the hell?" he said.

He took another slug of the whiskey, then put the bottle back into the pack. He looked in the general direction from which the sounds of the cattle came, north and a little west, in the mountains. That was puzzling.

Those mountains were too rough for cattle, too steep, and there was really no good grazing to attract them. Why would cows leave the easy grazing in lush grass down in the valley for these mountains? He wanted to investigate, but he knew that if he abandoned his packhorse with the fresh carcass on its back, he would be inviting some mountain lion to a bloody feast.

He decided to take a quick look anyway, then get right back to his packhorse. If what he found merited further investigation, he would take the packhorse and its load down to the ranch, then come back for a closer look. Reluctantly, he rode forward, leaving the packhorse behind.

He had not gone far when he found himself over-looking a deep and narrow box canyon. He dismounted and moved forward on foot until he was at the edge of the drop-off. On his belly, he crawled forward and stuck his head out over the edge. The sides of the canyon were incredibly steep, almost straight up and down, and it was a hell of a long drop from where he was to the bottom.

The canyon was crowded with cows. If the grass had been good when they got in there, he thought, it wouldn't last long. He wondered how they had gotten there and whose they might be. Were they some of Forrest Harper's cattle that had somehow wandered into this canyon from Harper's eastern range? Could they be the stolen cattle that had so mysteriously disappeared?

He backed up, stood up, and walked east, skirting the rim of the canyon, and then he could see, at the far western end of the canyon, the narrow gap through which the cattle had to have entered. It had been blocked by a man-made gate, and from his distance away from it, he couldn't be sure, but it looked to Slocum as if the gate had been deliberately hidden from view by carefully placed piles of brush.

He wanted to find his way on down into the canyon. He wanted to get a closer look at the cattle and check brands, but he remembered his elk and the packhorse, and he also told himself that before poking around any further into this new and extraordinary discovery, he ought to tell Happy about it. Although he couldn't imagine what it could be, there might be some logical explanation for the cows in the canyon. Reluctantly, he hurried back to his horse and mounted up.

16

After supper, back at the ranch house, Happy, Joy, and Slocum sat in easy chairs. Each had a glass of whiskey, and Slocum was smoking a cigar.

"Happy," said Slocum, "how well do you know Harper's layout?"

"What do you mean?" asked Happy. "I ain't rode his range, if that's what you mean. But really, there ain't that much difference in his land and mine. Both run from the road on the west to the base of the mountains to the east. North of here, to his south, we run into each other. Most of the land's flat, or nearly flat, and we're about equal with trees and water."

"Do your cattle ever get up into those mountains?"

"No. Hell no," said Happy. "They're steep and

150

rocky, and there ain't nothing for them to eat up there, anyhow.''

"Did you know that there was a box canyon just about behind Harper's house?''

"A box canyon? You mean back in those mountains?''

"With a real narrow gap that leads into it,'' said Slocum.

"I ain't never heard about it before,'' said Happy.

"Neither have I,'' said Joy.

"Well, it's back there. And right now, it's full of cattle, and the gap is closed, like the gate's been shut.''

"You mean there's cattle penned up in there?'' Joy asked.

"That's right.''

"That don't make sense,'' said Happy.

"No, it don't,'' said Slocum, "Unless they're stolen.''

"By God,'' said Happy, jumping to his feet. "That's it. That's where the damned stolen cattle got to. We'll ride out first thing in the morning and get a look at them.''

"Well,'' said Slocum, "you're the boss, but if it was up to me, I'd say let's just keep this information to ourselves for a little while. Just sit on it and see what happens.''

"What? How come?''

"I been thinking about that little canyon,'' said Slocum. "You know, you might've been wrong about

Jim Fuller, but then, me and the sheriff might've been wrong about Church, too. We might've been suckered again.''

"What're you getting at, Slocum?" asked Happy.

"I don't know," said Slocum. "But what if Church wasn't the rustler?"

"Well, then," said Happy, "I guess there'll be more cattle stole."

"And if the cattle I saw are the stolen cattle—"

"Then when the rustlers hit us again," said Joy, "they'll run the cows they steal this time in there with the others."

"Yeah. And if the rustlers are hiding the cows in that canyon," said Slocum, "they're going to have to move them out before much longer."

"And now that we know where they are," said Joy, "we'll be watching."

"Going in or coming out," said Happy, "we'll get them."

"Yeah," said Slocum. "That's just about the way I got it figured."

Slocum was just about to drift off to sleep, when he heard the knob of the door to his room being turned. His Colt was just beside the bed, and slowly, he slipped his right hand out from under the sheet to grip its handle. His thumb was in position to pull back the hammer.

Then the door opened, and a figure moved into the room and quietly closed the door again. Slocum couldn't make out who it was; it was too dark, but the intruder was being very quiet. He thought he knew, but just in case he should be wrong, he kept his hand on the Colt. Then he had the distinct feeling that someone was standing at the foot of his bed.

"Are you going to identify yourself," he asked in a low voice, "or I am going to have to shoot you?"

"Don't shoot me, John," whispered Joy. "At least not yet."

He felt a tugging at the sheets, and then he realized that she had crawled underneath the top sheet and was moving up between his legs. He let go of the Colt and lifted the sheet with both hands to look under it. It did no good. All he could see was black.

But he felt her hands sliding on his thighs, slowly moving up and up. Then her fingertips were tickling his balls, and something else down there began moving up, moving up, and swelling and throbbing. The fingers of her left hand gripped it hard and squeezed, and it bucked like a wild mustang. Her right hand moved in under his heavy balls and hefted them, as if she were testing their weight.

"Whoever you are," he said, "I hope you came into the right room."

For an answer, he received a quick lap on the head of his cock from a wet tongue, and his body gave an involuntary jerk. Then soft lips surrounded his cock and pressed it, then loosened a bit to slide down the shaft. The pressure was applied again, and the motion reversed. The lips were removed, the cock was released.

Joy crawled upward, licking Slocum's belly and chest, and then she was kissing his lips and thrusting her tongue into his hungry mouth. She slid off to one side to lie beside him, her back to him, her butt shoved against his body. He turned on his side and searched with his cock for her ready pussy. She reached around to give him a hand, and soon he slid easily into her damp tunnel. With his right arm, he reached around her and found a breast. Then he shoved himself into her, all the way, and she gasped.

They moved slowly, rhythmically, their bodies absolutely in tune with each other. It was quiet, and it was lovely, and when they came, they came together. In a moment, he went soft and slipped free, and Joy rolled over, her head on his chest. He cradled her in his left arm.

"John," she said, "that was wonderful."

"Yes," he said. "It was."

"I'm glad you're here."

"Um. Me, too."

"Are you really?"

"Yes. I am."

"Even with all the trouble?" she asked. "Happy lied to you to get you here, and then you've been beat up and shot at."

"That's one reason I stayed," he said. "I don't like being done that way. I didn't want to just let it go."

"You said that's one reason," she said. "Is there another?"

"Yes."

She waited for more, but he was silent. She wanted to hear more, but she didn't want to have to drag it out of him, and she didn't want him to say it if he didn't really mean it. She snuggled up against him. He squeezed her tight with both arms.

"You're the other reason," he said. "I, uh, I think I kind of like you."

Lying against him there in the dark, she smiled. She guessed that she would have to be content with that answer, at least for the time being.

17

Slocum wasn't too crazy about the big, happy crowd, but everyone else seemed to be having a roaring great time. Happy Kramer and Jim Fuller were getting on famously, and Forrest Harper was getting in on the act, too. There was plenty of everything for everybody to eat, and there was plenty of whiskey. Some of the cowboys were getting a little rowdy in their drunkenness, but it wasn't anything to worry about. They were just having a good time, and everyone seemed to think it was well deserved by all.

Curly, from Fuller's ranch, had brought a fiddle, and he began to play fast, happy dance tunes. Then Whitey Wilson surprised everyone by producing a harmonica and joining in on the music with Curly. When the tune was that of a song any of the cowboys knew the words to, they sang in loud voices, some off-key, a few on. A couple of the boys jumped up and danced, stamping and whooping to the music.

Joy was busy most of the time playing the hostess, but once or twice she let herself be caught by a cowboy wanting a dancing partner. In addition to the ranchers and cowboys from the three big ranches, there were guests from Dog Leg Creek, both men and women. Burl was even there. He had figured that all of his customers would be at the big doings at the Kramer Ranch anyway, so he just closed the saloon and headed out that way himself.

Slocum mixed a little at first, speaking to folks, engaging in brief conversations with a few, but mostly he sat back out of the way and watched, drinking whiskey alone. Laughing, whooping, and dancing was really not his style, although he could well understand why these folks all felt like letting off steam, what with Church and his gang of ruffians finally out of the way, and things patched up between Kramer and Fuller.

He particularly watched Forrest Harper. He wondered if Harper was aware of the box canyon east of his ranch and of the cows that were hidden back there. He had met Harper and liked him, and he had especially liked Harper's foreman, Billy Riles. He didn't really think that anything was wrong over there, or maybe he just didn't want to think so. After having made so many wrong-headed assumptions over the rustling, Slocum wasn't about to make another. There would be no more accusations until there was proof, at least as far as he was concerned.

Still, the only way to the entrance to the box canyon was through Harper's land, and just about the only way to get into and out of the canyon without Harper or some of his boys knowing about it, would be to slip in at night.

Slocum's glass was empty, and he got up from where he had been sitting on the edge of the porch to go find a bottle over at one of the long tables set up in the yard. He was pouring whiskey into his glass when Billy Riles stepped up beside him.

"Can I have a little of that good stuff?" said Riles.

"Sure," said Slocum, and he refilled the glass Riles had put on the table. "That's what it's here for."

"Hell of a party," said Riles.

"Yeah," said Slocum. "I guess."

"It don't suit your taste?" Riles asked.

"It don't need to," said Slocum. "It ain't for me."

"Well," said Riles, "I think I understand. I don't really care for this sort of thing myself. Don't get me wrong. I think it's great of old Happy and Miss Kramer to throw this whoop-de-do. Most everyone's having a fine time."

"Yeah," said Slocum. "They sure seem to be." He gestured toward the porch behind them. "Care to sit a spell?" he asked.

Riles followed Slocum over to the porch, and they sat down. Slocum produced a couple of cigars from his shirt pocket and offered one to Riles.

"Thanks," said Riles. He took the cigar. Slocum poked the other one into his own mouth, then took out his tin of matches. He picked a match out of the tin, struck it on the porch, and lit both smokes.

"Quite a celebration," said Riles. "Be a bunch of heads hurting in the morning. Not much work'll get done tomorrow, either."

"Yeah," said Slocum.

"Hell of a good reason for it, though," said Riles. "Three ranches been losing cattle. Now the rustlers're all dead or run off. I reckon that's cause enough for celebrating."

"You really think the rustlers are all gone?" asked Slocum.

"Don't you?"

"I don't know. No one's yet figured out whatever become of the stolen cattle."

"Well," said Riles, "I'd say that Church and his gang managed to get them out of this valley at night, right after they stole them, and sold them up north somewhere."

"Yeah," said Slocum. "I guess."

"You got any other explanation?" asked Riles.

"No, I sure don't," said Slocum. "You must be right."

But he really didn't think so. It would have been a damn good trick to get that many cows out of the valley without being seen or without having left any trail, even at night. Besides that, Slocum figured that the cows he had seen in the hidden canyon were more than likely all of the stolen cattle. If that was true, then none had been driven out of the valley. And the more Slocum thought about it, the more convinced he became that Church had not been the rustler, or if he had been involved, someone else had been behind it.

The party continued well into the night, and Slocum figured he wouldn't see Joy alone until well into the next day. Some of the cowboys had already passed out. They wouldn't be getting up to go home until noon. There wouldn't be much work done the next day, either.

"Well, hell," Slocum said to Riles, "I've seen about enough of this. I'm going to go get me some sleep."

Riles opined that was probably a pretty good idea, and he thought that he would go on home and do the same. He thanked Slocum kindly for the whiskey and the cigar and bade him good night. Slocum got up and went on into the house. For maybe a half hour after he had hit the sack, Slocum was kept awake by the whooping and hollering out in the yard. Then it ceased to bother him, and he drifted off to sleep.

The next morning, Slocum, having retired early, was up before anyone else. He went into the kitchen and fixed his own breakfast and coffee, and when he had done with it, he cleaned up the mess he had made, and then he went outside. Just as he had expected, there were cowboys lying around all over the yard.

Some of them were actually Kramer hands. The rest, the majority, would have to climb onto their horses and ride home with their hangovers.

Slocum walked out to the corral and caught his horse, saddled it, and rode off across the range, headed north and a little east. By the time he was riding alongside the base of the mountains and onto the eastern edge of Harper's spread, he figured the hungover cowboys would be just starting to stir out in the yard back at the Kramer house. That was just fine with him. He wanted to do some investigating, and he wanted to do it alone and unobserved, if possible.

He saw no cowboys out on the range, and he was pleased to observe that Harper's herd was not in the vicinity. If the cattle were grazing on some other part of the ranch, it was unlikely that he would see any cowboys at all. That was just the way he wanted it.

When he reached the general vicinity of the opening into the canyon, he rode slowly. He knew he would have to hunt for it. Riding along the valley's edge, the mountains rising sharply just to his right, he couldn't possibly tell exactly where he had been when he was looking down into the hidden canyon from above.

He investigated a couple of niches in the rocks that led him down false trails—short ones, fortunately. Then he almost rode past the entrance to the canyon. He would have missed it altogether had he not heard the cattle lowing. They sounded like they were in the bottom of a well. Slocum poked around in the brush until he found where the entrance to the canyon had been carefully masked. Pulling some of the camouflage out of the way, he rode in.

He found himself riding through a narrow passage with high, steep walls, a natural corridor that eventually led him to what appeared to be a dead end. Again he pulled aside some brush, and he found the gate, the one he had looked down on before. He dismounted and tied his horse. Then he dragged the gate open enough to allow him to slip in.

The first brand he saw was Happy Kramer's. He kept looking, and after having seen several more of Happy's, he found some of Fuller's and a few of Harper's cows. He also noted that the grass in the canyon floor was just about gone. These cattle would have to be moved, and soon.

When Slocum left the canyon, he was careful to put everything back pretty much as he had found it. He rode back the same way he had come, and again, he saw no cowboys. He felt almost certain that no one had seen him.

Back at the ranch house, he found Happy up and groaning, a glass of whiskey in his hand.

"Hair of the dog," said Happy.

Joy was in the kitchen preparing breakfast. Slocum poked his head through the door.

"What're we having?" he asked. "Eggs and bacon or last night's leftovers?"

"Leftovers, hell," said Joy. "Those cowboys ate up everything in sight. I know it's lunchtime, but I'm cooking breakfast. You want some?"

"Sure," he said. He got a cup of coffee and went back into the living room. He sat down in a chair just across from where Happy sat moaning, and he lit himself a cigar.

"God damn, Happy," he said. "You look like hell. Can't take it anymore?"

"Shut up, you smart aleck bastard," said Happy. "What makes you so damn chipper, anyway?"

"I quit early last night," said Slocum. "Showed some good sense. Unlike some other folks I know."

"I couldn't very well quit early when I was the host, now could I?" said Happy. "Some of us around here has got duties and responsibilities, a certain position in the community to uphold. You wouldn't know about those kinds of things, though, would you?"

"No," said Slocum. "I reckon not." He puffed at his cigar contentedly.

"All right then," said Happy. "So don't give me any more of your smart alecky lip. Let me suffer in peace."

"I do know something about stolen cows, though," said Slocum.

"What?"

"I went out for a long ride this morning, while you were still sound asleep."

"Where?" said Happy. "What did you find?"

"I ain't telling you nothing," said Slocum. "Not till you're in fit shape to listen to it."

"The hell you say," roared Happy, and his own outburst caused him to fall back in his chair with a groan. "Ah, my head. See what you're causing now?"

"Have some breakfast and some coffee," said Slocum. "Then we'll talk."

Happy's disposition was considerably improved by a full belly, and after several cups of coffee, he walked outside with Slocum. They sat on the edge of the porch.

"Now, are you going to talk to me?" asked Happy.

"I found the way into the canyon," said Slocum, "and I checked the cattle in there. They're the stolen cattle, all right. There were animals in there with all three brands, yours, Fuller's, and Harper's."

"By damn," said Happy. "Let's go get them."

"Not so fast. There are still some questions."

"Like?"

"Like, who put them in there?" said Slocum. "If Church found that place and hid the cattle in there, then he had to move them a long way around Fuller's and do it at night to keep from being seen. That don't hardly seem likely to me. Course, it is possible, I guess, and if Church did do it, then you and me are the only ones around who know they're in there, and if we don't get them out pretty damn soon, they're going to start to go hungry."

"All right then," said Happy, "what's the rest of your reasoning?"

"Well, suppose Church ain't the one. Suppose it was someone else."

"Who?"

"That's what we want to find out, now, ain't it?" said Slocum. "And we ain't going to find out by letting on that we know or by turning them cows out of the canyon."

"So what do we do?"

"Wait just a few more days," said Slocum. "If the rustlers are still around, they'll have to be moving those cows out soon. If we hide and watch, we might just catch them red-handed."

Between the two of them, Slocum and Happy decided that Sully Nolan, Monk Barnett, Audie Paget, A. G. Spalding, Pudge Camp, and Whitey Wilson were absolutely trustworthy. Of course, they had been fooled before, and they really had no idea who the rustlers were, but then they were going to have to trust someone and take a chance. The two of them couldn't watch the canyon alone around the clock.

Sully gathered up the crew, and Happy told them of the discovery and of the plan. He emphasized the need for absolute secrecy. Then Slocum led them all to the canyon by way of the mountain trail.

"We'll watch from up here," he said. "If anyone saw us down below, they'd just ride on by and not give themselves away."

"Say I'm up here watching," said Sully, "and I

see a bunch of rustlers open up that gate and start to move the cattle out. What do I do then? By the time I could get back down to the ranch, they'd be long gone.''

"There's nine of us here," said Slocum. "We'll watch in teams of three. If we see them start to move the cattle out, one will stay here and watch the way they go. You can see a hell of a long way from here. Another one'll ride down the mountain and follow the herd, keeping back a safe distance. The third will ride for the rest of us back at the ranch."

"All right," said Sully. "Who're the teams and who has the first watch?"

Slocum, Sully, and Monk stayed behind while the rest returned to the ranch. They spent a slow, boring eight hours watching the cattle below. At last their relief came in the form of Happy, Joy, and Whitey. The tired first team rode back to the ranch to get some sleep. In another eight hours, Slocum was awake to see the third team, consisting of A. G., Pudge, and Audie, head out. Eight more uneventful hours passed, and Slocum and his team headed back up the mountain trail.

"You really think this is going to do any good, Slocum?" asked Sully, as they rode along the ridge. "Setting up on the mountain, watching some cows?"

"I don't know," said Slocum. "If old Church really was the rustler, or the head of the rustlers, then it damn sure ain't going to do us no good. But if it wasn't him, if it's someone else, then we ought to catch the bastards like this, sooner or later. They'll have to get back to those cows.''

When at last they reached the campsite, Audie came rushing to meet them.

''What's up, boy?'' asked Sully.

''We got some action,'' said Audie. ''Not enough to come arunning, but we sure got something to report.''

''What happened?'' Slocum asked.

''One lone rider went into the canyon,'' said Audie. ''And he for sure knew what he was doing. He rode straight to the entrance, and he looked around like he didn't want to be seen. Then he moved brush and rode in. At this end of the passageway, he moved more brush and opened the gate. He went in and looked around awhile. Then he rode on back out again.''

''That's all?'' said Sully.

''That's all.''

''Likely he was checking the grass,'' said Slocum. ''They can't keep those cows in there much longer. My guess is that he'll be back tonight with more riders and they'll start to move them out. I don't suppose you could identify the rider?''

''No,'' said Audie. ''Not from up here.''

''Or the horse?''

Audie shook his head. ''Nope,'' he said. ''Afraid not.''

''Where did he go when he rode out of the canyon?'' Slocum asked.

"Straight on over into Dog Leg Creek," said Audie.

"Damn," said Slocum. "That's no help. Well, all right. You all go on back down to the ranch. All we can do now is just stick to the original plan."

"So nothing's changed?" said Sully, getting down off his horse's back. "We're still just setting up here on our tired ass waiting for something to happen."

Slocum swung down out of the saddle.

"Just one thing's changed," he said. "I think they'll be moving them out real soon now."

18

When Audie Paget, A. G. Spalding, and Pudge Camp got down onto flat land, Audie turned his horse north.

"Hey, Audie," said Pudge, "where you going?"

"I'm going to town," said Audie. "See you fellows later."

"Now what the hell do you reckon he's up to?" said Pudge.

"I don't know," said A. G., "and I don't give a shit. I'm going back to the bunkhouse and get myself some shut-eye. I ain't been the same since that big party the other night."

Audie rode into town casually. He nodded or smiled at folks he knew or just recognized, and he pulled up in front of the saloon. His intention was to appear to have no purpose other than getting a glass of whiskey. In reality, he had a very definite purpose.

He had told the truth to Slocum and the others when he had said that he could not identify the rider he had seen go into the canyon. But he was pretty sure the man had been wearing a blue shirt and a dark hat and riding a black horse. And he had gone to Dog Leg Creek. Audie had not wanted to say anything until he was sure, but he thought that if he found the man in town, he would know it was the same rider.

As he dismounted, Audie heard a distant roll of thunder. He looked up into the sky and saw, to the west, heavy, dark clouds moving toward the valley. He walked on into the saloon.

"Audie," said Burl. "What brings you in here this time of day?"

"Just a little glass of whiskey," said Audie.

"What's the matter? Did we drink it all up out there at the ranch the other night?"

"Hell," said Audie, "how would I know? On a normal day like this, they won't let me into the big house to see if there's whiskey or not. Won't let me anywhere near it. Pour me a shot, will you?"

He tossed a coin onto the bar, and Burl put a glass in front of him, then poured it full. He pushed the coin back toward Audie.

"This one's on the house, Audie," he said.

"Why, thank you, Burl."

"Hell, I drank enough of your boss's whiskey at the big hooraw," said Burl.

Audie gave a short laugh, then lifted the whiskey to his lips and drank down about half the shot. He put the glass back down and shook his head.

"Whew," he said.

"That's good stuff," said Burl.

"I reckon," said Audie. "Say, Burl, any of the other boys been in yet today?"

"Oh, Billy Riles came in, but he just had a cup of coffee and left."

"Oh, yeah? What was he wearing?"

"Blue shirt, I think. Yeah. Blue. What the hell you want to know that for?"

"Help me spot him," said Audie. "I need to see him about something."

Audie finished his drink and turned to leave the saloon.

"Thanks for the whiskey, Burl."

"Audie," said Burl.

"Yeah?"

"When Billy left here, I was over by the window cleaning a table. You might have to wait a spell to see him."

"How's that?"

"He met his boss out there on the walk. They went into the bank together."

Audie looked through the front window of the bank, but he saw no sign of either Forrest Harper or Billy Riles. A big black horse wearing a Harper brand was tied to the hitching rail in front, though. Standing next to it was a roan, and Audie looked for the brand it carried. Harper. He walked to the corner of the bank building and slipped around.

Marvin Oats's office window was just down there near the back corner. Keeping as quiet as he could, Audie made his way to the window and leaned up against the wall. Fortunately, it was a warm day, and the window was opened. He recognized Oats's voice.

"The agents will be here next week," Oats was saying, "and then the cat'll be out of the bag. If you're going to make a move, you'd better make it fast."

"If we hit them one more time, and hit them hard," said Harper, "I think they'll sell. But we've got to move those cattle out of the canyon first."

"Won't it be risky to move the cattle first?" said Oats. "Someone might see you."

"We can get them out at night," said Riles.

"Everyone's relaxed now, what with Church being killed. They won't be watching, especially at night. Then the next night we can hit both ranches, burn the ranch houses, and run off the cattle."

"What's it going to look like if the other two get burned out and you're untouched?" asked Oats.

"Hell," said Riles, "that's easy. We'll run. off some of our own cattle, and we'll fire the bunkhouse. We'll tell a tale about how we fought off a bunch of riders in the night."

"Then you'll make the offers on the Kramer and Fuller ranches," said Harper. "Not me. They won't know that I had anything to do with it. I'll even tell them that you made me an offer, too.''

There was a loud clap of thunder just then, and Audie felt a heavy raindrop fall between his shoulder blades.

"We're in for a storm,'' he heard Oats say, and in another few seconds, someone slammed the window down tight. Then the rain started in earnest, and Audie turned to run back toward the street.

"Damn,'' he said.

The mountainside was treacherous in the driving rain, and it took Audie almost twice as long as normal to make it to the top. He was getting a good soaking, in spite of the slicker he had pulled out of his blanket roll.

At the campsite he found the three watchmen on duty huddled beneath a makeshift lean-to behind a small fire. He hoped they had some coffee going in there. He dismounted quickly and ran for the shelter.

"Audie,'' said Sully. "What the hell're you doing back here?''

"I found him,'' said Audie. "I found the son of a bitch—and even more.''

"What are you talking about?'' said Slocum.

"The rider in the blue shirt,'' said Audie, "the one who rode into the canyon. I went into town and found him. It was Billy Riles.''

"Riles?'' said Sully.

"Are you sure?'' asked Slocum.

"Just as sure as I'm soaked to the bone," said Audie. "You got any coffee left in that pot?"

Slocum poured a cup of coffee and handed it to Audie.

"Thanks," said Audie. He took a sip.

"What about Riles?" said Sully.

"He went into the bank and met with his boss and old Oats in Oats's office. I sneaked up to the window for a listen. There's some railroad men coming to town next week, and Oats is going to try to buy out Kramer and Fuller. I couldn't hear everything, but I figure they're planning to sell to the railroad."

"Son of a bitch," said Sully.

"Wait," said Audie. "That ain't all. They said they was going to move the cattle out tonight, and then tomorrow night they're going to hit us and Fuller. They're going to burn the houses and run off the cattle."

"The dirty bastards," said Monk.

"They mean to get Happy and Mr. Fuller hurting so bad that they'll sell," said Audie. "Only it won't be Harper who makes the offer. It'll be the banker, Oats. Then he'll sell to the railroad men. I guess Harper's going to get his share later. Only thing is, this rain started up while they was talking. You think they'll try to move them cows out tonight after all?"

"They'd be damn fools to try it," said Monk.

"Well, hell," said Slocum, "why don't we move them out?"

"What?" said Sully.

"Let's just go down there and turn the bastards loose onto Harper's range," said Slocum. "Then let's get back to the ranch and tell Happy what the hell's going on."

19

It didn't take much persuasion to get the cattle moving out of the canyon and onto the open, grassy range of the Harper Ranch. Audie and Monk stayed out on the flat in case any Harper cowboys happened along, but none did. When the last of the cattle were out in the open, Slocum and the others headed for the Kramer ranch house.

They filled Happy in with all the information Audie had picked up in town, and then they told him what they had done and why. They figured that the rain was going to play hell with the plans of Harper and Riles anyhow, so they had turned the cattle out. The crooks might find out about the cattle soon, and they might not. Either way, and in spite of the rain, Slocum suggested that they gather up their forces, their own and those of Jim Fuller, if he was willing, and ride straight against Harper before he realized that they were onto his game.

"Get everyone armed and mounted, Happy," said Slocum. "I'll ride over to Fuller's and tell him what's up."

"We'll meet you in the road by Harper's main gate," said Happy. "Come on, Sully. Let's get the boys ready."

Slocum left Fuller's place with Jim Fuller riding right beside him. Behind them were a dozen cowboys. In a few minutes they joined the Kramer band already gathered at the gate to Harper's and waiting for them.

"Let's hit them," shouted Happy, and he kicked his horse and raced through the gate, the small army right behind him. The driving rain hampered their vision, but it would do the same to the men at Harper's. It would also muffle the sound of the pounding hoofs of their horses.

Because of the rain, they were close to the ranch house before they saw it. As soon as it came into Happy's view, he shouted out an order.

"Spread out," he roared, and his army formed itself into an arced line there in front of Harper's house. "Harper," Happy called. "Harper. You want to surrender or get wiped out?"

The door opened, and Harper stepped out onto his porch. He squinted into the heavy rain.

"Happy?" he said. "Happy, is that you?"

"It's me, you son of a bitch."

"What's this all about? Who're all those men with you?"

"It's all of my own crew and all of Fuller's," said Happy. "We ain't here to talk. Come out with your hands up—all of you—or we'll come ashooting."

Billy Riles came out of the house to stand beside his boss.

"What's going on?" he said.

"We know about the cows in the canyon," said Happy, "and we know all about you and Oats and the fucking railroad scheme, too."

Riles jerked his revolver and fired a shot that smashed into Happy's left shoulder. Then Riles and Harper ran back into the house, slamming the door behind them. Happy clutched his shoulder, fighting to maintain control of his horse, as all around him, men drew guns and fired at the house.

A Fuller cowboy fell from his horse, landing with a splash on the rain-soaked ground.

"Move back," shouted Slocum. "Move back."

The riders backed up, and the shooting slowed down.

"What now?" asked Fuller.

"Get someone to take Happy back home," said Slocum.

"I'll have a couple of my boys take him to my house," said Fuller. "It's closer."

"Sully," said Slocum, "get these boys to spread

out more, and tell them not to shoot unless they've got something to shoot at.''

Another round of shots came at them, but it didn't come from the main house. Slocum pointed to his left.

"The bunkhouse," he said. Several cowboys to his left began peppering the front wall of the bunkhouse with bullets. Two men came running around one end of the bunkhouse, and two more from around the other end. They were all four dropped by Kramer and Fuller cowboys.

Suddenly there was no more shooting.

"What's going on?" said Sully.

"Maybe we got them all," said A. G.

"Hell," said Audie, "we didn't get them all. The only ones we even seen was the four that come outside.''

Then a stick with a white rag tied on its end was poked out a broken window on the front of the bunkhouse and waved.

"Don't shoot," someone yelled from behind the flag.

Slocum looked from the flag to the main house.

"Sully," he said, "take some boys over to the bunkhouse. Be careful. It might be a trick. Tell them if they come out with their hands up and no guns, they won't be hurt."

"What are you going to be doing?" asked Sully.

"Harper and Riles are in the house here," said

Slocum. "I'm going to try to figure out how to get them."

Slocum kept his eye on the main house, while Sully led some men over closer to the bunkhouse.

"Come on out with your hands up," Sully yelled. "No guns."

"Don't shoot," someone pleaded from inside.

"You come out with your hands in the air," said Sully, "and no one will get shot."

After a brief pause, the door of the bunkhouse was pushed open, and one cowboy came timidly out into the rain, his hands up beside his ears.

"Come on," said Sully. "Keep coming."

When fifteen men were lined up in front of the bunkhouse, Sully moved in closer.

"Is anyone else in there?" he said.

"No," said one of the captured cowboys. "We're all there is."

Sully turned to two men beside him.

"Go in there and check it out," he said. "Be careful."

The two men went inside. A moment later one of them looked back out the door.

"It's all clear in here," he said.

Slocum was aware of what had happened at the bunkhouse, so he knew that the battle had been won. But they had heard nothing from Harper or Riles. The two men were, as far as he knew, still inside the ranch house. They could have run out the back door, but there was no place for them to go out there. The corral with the horses was in plain view of Slocum and the Kramer-Fuller band. Behind the house was nothing but open grassland and a long walk to the mountains.

"Harper," he shouted.

There was no answer.

"Riles."

Still no answer. Slocum glanced to his immediate left and saw Monk Barnett standing there. He knew already that Audie was just to his right. Other men were spread out in both directions from there.

"Audie," Slocum said, "Monk, let's all move in on them."

Slowly the line of cowboys sloshed through the mud toward the ranch house. With each step, Slocum anticipated a shot from a window. None came. Soon he was standing just by the porch.

"Harper," he shouted.

Still there was no answer, and Slocum stepped up onto the porch. Audie followed, and they moved to the door. Slocum looked at Audie as he reached for the doorknob. He tried it and it turned. Stepping to the side of the door, he shoved the door into the house. There was no response, no shots, no voice. He looked at Audie, and Audie shrugged. Monk stepped up on the porch with them.

Slocum thumbed back the hammer of his Colt, then rushed inside. Poised to defend himself, he stopped still. Audie came in to stand on one side of him and Monk on the other. They stood there, unbelieving, staring at the bloody bodies of Harper and Riles lying on the floor just beneath the front window. Both had been killed in that first wild volley of shots from outside.

The captured cowboys claimed that they had nothing to do with the rustling and knew nothing of the grand scheme to acquire the valley to sell to the railroad. The four dead cowboys, they said, the ones who had put up a fight, had been close to Riles, and had probably been in on the plans. There was, of course, no way of knowing whether or not they told the truth. Jim Fuller told them to gather up their belongings and get the hell out of the country, far out, and they all agreed and lit out in a hurry.

Then Fuller, Slocum, Sully, Audie, and Monk rode into town. They left their horses standing in the rain in front of the bank and went inside. Fuller led the way into Oats's office against the protests of a teller behind a cage, and the five grim-faced men lined up in front of the startled banker's desk.

"What's the meaning of this?" said the banker.

"We ain't got a sheriff in this town right now," said Fuller, "so we've come to put you under arrest."

"What?" blustered Oats. "This is absurd. On what authority? On what charge?"

Slocum pulled out his Colt and cocked it.

"This is the authority," he said, watching Oats's face fade to even whiter.

"Conspiracy," said Fuller. "Intent to defraud me and Happy Kramer out of our land. Cattle rustling and murder. There might be some more after we think about it for awhile."

"Come on," said Slocum.

"Where are you taking me?"

"To the jailhouse," said Fuller. "We'll figure out some way to have a trial."

"You just wait until Forrest Harper hears about this," said Oats, as Monk dragged him from behind his desk.

"Harper's dead," said Audie. "So's Riles and four other Harper men. The rest has lit out for the far horizon."

"You're all alone, Oats," said Slocum. "Let's go."

At the Kramer ranch house, Happy was propped up in bed on several pillows. A glass was in his right hand and a whiskey bottle on the bedside table within easy reach. His shoulder was bandaged and his left arm wrapped tightly against his body. Slocum and Joy were in the room with him.

"We thought you might be interested in the latest word from town," said Slocum.

"What's that?" said Happy.

"Well, it seems that last night, the word having got around town about Oats's involvement with Harper, some unknown, or at least unnamed folks took it on themselves to see justice done. They dragged our

local banker out of jail and took him out to the nearest tall oak tree.''

"Strung him up, did they?" said Happy.

"I understand he's hanging there yet," said Slocum.

"Well, I'll be damned," said Happy. He took another slug of whiskey. "I wonder if they held a trial
for the poor man."

"I don't know," said Slocum, "but if they did,
they sure as hell found him guilty."

Happy chuckled and took another drink.

"Well," he said, "I'd say this calls for another
celebration. Wouldn't you?"

"You're not fit for one," said Joy.

"Well then, when I get a little more of my
strength back. It won't be long. Will you still be
here, Slocum?"

"I don't know," said Slocum. "My job's done.
The thing you hired me for has been taken care of."

"Did I ever say that I was hiring you to take care
of rustlers?"

"Hell no," said Slocum. "You—"

"Then how do you know the job is over? Didn't I
tell you that you could stay here for as long as you
liked? Well, I meant it."

Joy took hold of Slocum's arm and moved her
body up close against his.   "I wish you'd stay,"
she said. "We might just go ahead and have a celebration. A private one, quiet, just you and me."

Happy's face flushed, and he reached for his whiskey bottle.

"Well," said Slocum, "maybe I will stick around, for a while at least. See how things work out. I might just find out that I like it around here."